"Oh, look, Sam, look at it!" Max jumped up and threw her arms around him. "Did you see it? I can't believe I found it!" She was laughing and crying and kissing him.

Sam caught her to him. "I like it," he said, grinning as she planted more kisses all over his face. "I think you missed a spot right here," he added, pointing to his chin. "Now it's my turn," he said, leaning down to drop a kiss on her cheek, another on her chin. Another on the corner of her mouth.

But his kisses weren't quick, the gift of an exuberant spirit. They were promises of things to come. His mouth slanted over hers with a hunger that was palpable. Warmth flooded her whole body, making her desperate to increase the delicious sensations.

"Touch me, Angel," he said. "I think I'll die if I can't feel your hand on my skin."

A surge of desire poured through her. . . .

WHAT ARE *LOVESWEPT* ROMANCES?

They are stories of true romance and touching emotion. We believe those two very important ingredients are constants in our highly sensual and very believable stories in the *LOVESWEPT* line. Our goal is to give you, the reader, stories of consistently high quality that may sometimes make you laugh, sometimes make you cry, but are always fresh and creative and contain many delightful surprises within their pages.

Most romance fans read an enormous number of books. Those they truly love, they keep. Others may be traded with friends and soon forgotten. We hope that each *LOVESWEPT* romance will be a treasure—a "keeper." We will always try to publish

LOVE STORIES YOU'LL NEVER FORGET
BY AUTHORS YOU'LL ALWAYS REMEMBER

The Editors

LOVESWEPT® • 293

Jan Hudson

Water Witch

BANTAM BOOKS
TORONTO • NEW YORK • LONDON • SYDNEY • AUCKLAND

WATER WITCH

A Bantam Book / November 1988

If you would be interested in receiving protective vinyl covers for your Loveswept books, please write to this address for information:

*Loveswept
Bantam Books
P.O. Box 985
Hicksville, NY 11802*

ISBN 0-553-21945-6

Published simultaneously in the United States and Canada

Bantam Books are published by Bantam Books, a division of Bantam Doubleday Dell Publishing Group, Inc. Its trademark, consisting of the words "Bantam Books" and the portrayal of a rooster, is Registered in U.S. Patent and Trademark Office and in other countries. Marca Registrada. Bantam Books, 666 Fifth Avenue, New York, New York 10103.

PRINTED IN THE UNITED STATES OF AMERICA

O 0 9 8 7 6 5 4 3 2 1

To Joyce Flaherty, special lady.
And with thanks to Traye Phelps
of Phelps Drilling Company,
Carla Edson, Bill Page, and all the other nice
folks in Kerrville for their help.

One

Flickering lights from the television cast eerie shadows on the walls of the room. Max Strahan lay in bed, her head propped against a pile of pillows, her hands clutching a bowl of popcorn, her eyes glued to the TV set. As she watched the grotesque shape on the screen rise from the swamp and drag itself through the woods, chills rippled up her spine. Her heart began to pound in tempo with the creepy background music as the muck-covered monster made its way toward the darkened house.

A banging noise outside startled her, and she nearly jumped out of her skin. She tensed, every sense alert. The Doberman lying beside her whined and burrowed his head under her arm. When she realized what had made the sound, she laughed and gave the dog a swat. "Oh, Dowser, you big chicken. It was just a tree limb blowing against the house. Hush. We're just getting to the good part."

Max grabbed a handful of popcorn and munched

wide-eyed as the violins continued their suspenseful strains. She trembled as the heavy-breathing creature dragged itself toward its destination, leaving a dripping trail behind.

Dowser whined and burrowed deeper.

Max knew she shouldn't be watching this old horror picture. She knew she'd probably have nightmares—especially in an isolated, unfamiliar house in a strange town. She didn't know a soul in the Texas hill country, unless she counted the kid who'd filled up the Charger at the gas station this afternoon.

Had she locked the doors? Of course she had. The little one-story stone and cedar house beside the meandering river was snug. After she'd locked her truck in the attached garage, she remembered carefully locking the kitchen door behind her. She'd also bolted the front door and turned on the porch light to push away the shadows made by the huge, spreading live oaks sheltering the place. A lamp still burned in the rustic yet expensively furnished living room. It was ridiculous to allow herself to imagine that a swamp monster might be lurking in the Guadalupe River.

Wasn't it?

Of course it was. It was absolutely silly to lie here in this antique four-poster and allow herself to be scared witless. Max knew she should get up right now and turn off the set. But she couldn't. She was addicted to scary films—a monster movie junkie.

And anyway, she thought, drawing the covers around her and scrunching deeper into the pillows, she didn't want to get up. Who knew what might be under the bed?

Mesmerized, one arm around the nervous Doberman and the other around the popcorn bowl, Max watched the slimy monster slip into the house and trudge up the stairs to the little girl's room. The only sound was its labored, guttural rasping.

As the creature slowly pushed open the door, Max gave a little squeal and covered her face with her hands. Hairs prickled on the back of her neck as she peeked through her fingers at the blond child innocently sleeping in her bed, not knowing that the ghoulish threat stood only a few feet away, its bulging eyes glowing green as it beheld its next victim.

"Oh, I can't watch," Max whispered, turning away from the action on the screen. As her anxious gaze fell on the window of the bedroom, her eyes widened even farther and she sucked in a gasp. The sash was slowly rising and a man's leg slipped over the sill.

A piercing shriek ripped from her throat. Popcorn and pillows flew into the air as Max jumped from the bed and dashed across the room. She slammed the window down on the man's shin and yelled, "Get him, Dowser!"

The big hulk of a man outside was shouting and swearing and struggling to raise the window. Max held it down with every ounce of strength she possessed.

"Dowser!" she yelled again. "Help me!"

Dowser whined from under the bed.

"You cowardly disposal, I'm sending you to the pound tomorrow!"

His whining escalated to a mournful howl—still from under the bed.

Even though she was strong, Max was giving out. The quivering in her arms meant she couldn't hold on much longer. Had the intruder the advantage of both feet on the ground, she wouldn't have been a match for his brute force. Only an adrenaline rush gave her the strength she wielded. The man roared with fury as he strained against her. Besides a string of virulent oaths, she only managed to catch the words "damned idiot" and "breaking my leg."

"Pervert!" she screamed back at him.

Looking around frantically for some kind of weapon, Max spied her geologist's tool bag resting against the dresser. Still holding on to the window, she maneuvered until she could hook her toe around the strap and drag it toward her. Despite her best efforts, she felt the window give a fraction of an inch, then another.

She jumped and shoved down, hanging her whole weight on the window and kicking at the fingers that were winning the struggle against hers.

"Son of a bitch!" he yelled, falling back with a thud and more curses.

"Thank God," Max whispered as she realized the resistance had ceased. He'd fallen down. With his leg still trapped in the window, he wouldn't be able to get up easily. Now was her chance.

She upended the tool bag and grabbed a rock hammer and a spad. She pounded the naillike spad into one side of the window facing, snatched up another and drove it into the other side. For good measure, she picked up a third and nailed his pants leg to the sill.

"How do you like them apples, smart guy?" she said as she slapped the size twelve shoe protruding into her bedroom.

Still clutching the rock hammer, Max turned and glared at Dowser, who had inched his head from under the bed and was staring up at her with soulful eyes.

"You can come out now. I'll protect you from the big bad man."

Never lifting his head from the floor, Dowser scooted toward Max. His whimper was pitiful and pleading.

"All right. I'll forgive you." She reached down to scratch his ears. "Come on, let's call the police." Turning toward the window she shouted, "I'm calling the police!"

"Good!" the man outside yelled back, then began another round of blistering oaths.

After she made the phone call, Max sat down at the oak table in the kitchen, and began to shake. She clenched her hands and took a few deep breaths to gain control. "Don't fall apart now," she said, gritting her teeth. She could handle this. Like an affirmation, Max began to sing the familiar words of Helen Reddy's hit, "I Am Woman." She *was* strong, she told herself as she sang. And she *could* do anything.

It was less than five minutes before one of Kerr County's finest came roaring up the drive, lights flashing and siren screaming. Max ran out onto the porch to meet the officer. He got out of the car, grabbed his flashlight, and drew his gun.

"He's around there, officer," Max said, pointing to the side of the cottage.

"You stay in the house, ma'am. I'll check it out. We've had some trouble with a burglar in this area. And from all accounts, he's mean and he's slick."

"Oh, he's not going anywhere," Max said as she trailed along behind him toward where the man lay muttering. "I've got him nailed to the wall."

The deputy passed the beam of his flashlight over the prone figure with one leg stuck in the window. Max noticed that he was wearing a dark suit and tie. He seemed awfully well dressed for a burglar. Come to think of it, she remembered the big foot in her bedroom having on a hand-sewn Italian shoe. Very peculiar.

" 'Evening, Sam," the burly cop said with obvious amusement. He holstered his gun and gave a tug at his hat. "Looks like you got yourself in a predicament."

"Don't say another word, Dick Ware. Not another word," the man said fiercely. "Just help me get my leg out of this damned window. I think it's broken."

Puzzled, Max looked from one man to the other. "You know this trespasser, officer?"

"I'm not the trespasser, dammit!" Sam bellowed. "You are!"

"I am not. I have every right to be here. Buck Barton gave me the key. *I* came in the front door. *I* didn't try to climb through the window at midnight."

"Look," Sam said, "can we get my foot out of the window before we discuss this?"

Max turned to the deputy, who was snickering. "I don't think he's too dangerous, ma'am. You go raise the window and I'll get him on his feet."

"Who is he?" she asked Dick Ware.

"I'm Sam Garrett," the man on the ground answered. "Buck Barton's nephew. Now go raise the damned window!"

"Okay, okay," she said, and went inside.

Buck Barton's nephew? Dear Lord, she'd done it now. A sickening dread filled her. Had she blown the whole deal? She had to have this project. She was down to her last fifty-seven dollars and her charge card was to the limit. Already she'd sold her car and most of her furniture, and the mortgage payment was a month overdue. She couldn't lose everything. She just *couldn't.*

Even though the late September night was pleasantly cool, Max had broken out in a sweat by the time she retrieved her rock hammer and went to the window. Sticking the pick end through the eye of one of the spads, she gave a yank.

Stupid, Max, stupid, she berated herself in the same tone her father had always used. You always manage to screw things up. She pried out the other spad from the window and knelt to remove the one skewering his pants. Maybe she could make Sam Garrett understand—

"Would you hurry up!" she heard him yell.

She sighed, pulled out the last spad, and raised the window. Slowly she walked to the living room and waited for the inevitable.

Breathing fire, Sam Garrett limped onto the porch and jerked open the door. His leg wasn't broken, but it was throbbing like hell. He was going to tear a strip off of that little gal and toss her out on her—

He stopped cold. A tall, sloe-eyed angel with long legs and golden skin stood across the room wringing her hands, looking as if she were about to cry. She had high cheekbones and full lips and a little dent in her chin that didn't quite make a dimple. And she had a body that wouldn't quit.

With the light to her back, the thin white nightshirt she wore didn't leave much to the imagination. Given the fix he'd been in earlier, he hadn't paid much attention to what she looked like. And he couldn't see much of her in the dark outside.

But he could see her now. A different throb began to replace the one in his leg.

He tried to say something, but his mouth was dry and the words got stuck in his throat. He could only stand and stare at the outline of her breasts as they rose and fell with each rapid breath. He could see the dark shadows of her nipples beneath the sheer fabric, and a silky lock of honey-blond hair draped over her shoulder and curled just above the peak of the left one.

"Mr. Garrett?"

Sam forced his gaze to her face. When she licked her lips he heard a roaring in his ears and licked his own.

"Mr. Garrett?"

"Sam," he said. "Call me Sam."

Max's unblinking gaze traveled his length from head to foot and back again. Sam Garrett was a big one, she thought. At least six feet four, he was slim-hipped and square-jawed, and his shoulders seemed to fill the door frame. He had a ruddy, weathered complexion which had probably sported a mass of freckles as a kid, and a shock of deep auburn hair, thick and unruly, fell in a wave across his forehead. Power radiated from him like a generator. Here was a man used to calling all the shots. Under other circumstances she might have found him fascinating. He was some kind of a hunk—and she suspected he knew it—but now, all she could think of was that her only hope was about to go down the tubes.

She met his squint-eyed stare and swallowed. "Where's the deputy?"

"Gone," Sam said, still staring at her as if he were about to eat her alive.

Max wrung her hands and swallowed again. "Do you need to go to a hospital? How bad is your leg?"

"My leg?"

"Yes, your leg . . . the window . . . your leg."

"Oh, my leg," Sam said as if coming out of a fog. Glancing down, he lifted his foot and bent his knee a couple of times, testing. "It's just a little bruised, skinned up some maybe." He looked up and flashed a sexy, lopsided grin. "Angel, to make up for it you could probably kiss it and make it better."

Her jaw dropped, then her eyes narrowed as fury flashed through her. With clenched fists on her hips and feet planted apart, Max glared at him. "It'll be a cold day in hell, Mr. Garrett. What do you mean by breaking into my bedroom and scaring the pants off me?"

Sam's grin widened as his gaze swept her figure, revealed even more clearly with the stance she'd adopted. His gaze rested at the juncture of her legs. "Oh, is that where they went?"

Max drew her brows in a puzzled frown and looked down at herself. Mortification pulled the blood from her face. Dear Lord, she was nearly naked as a jaybird. With all the excitement, she'd forgotten that she was clad only in a short batiste nightshirt.

When he chuckled, she glared at him again.

"Ohhhhh, you . . . you . . ." Turning, she stomped into the bedroom and slammed the door so hard, all thirteen of Mrs. Barton's bluebonnet paintings rattled on the walls.

Dowser looked up from under the bed and she could have sworn he grinned. She scowled at him.

Rummaging through her suitcase, Max found a pair of cotton panties and pulled them on. She located a long plaid robe in the closet and donned it, muttering invectives against Sam Garrett as she snapped every snap from throat to hem. When she was done, she grabbed Dowser's collar and hauled him up. "Come on, you lily-livered beast. At least you can pretend to be a watchdog. Heel!"

Max reached for the doorknob, knowing it was too much to hope that Sam Garrett might be gone. She was right. He sat sprawled in a chintz-covered chair, his big foot propped on a matching ottoman, his pants leg pulled up to reveal a nasty scrape on his shin. Already it was turning various shades of purple. The moment she saw his leg, Max's righteous indignation dissolved.

"That looks awful. Let me get the first-aid kit." Turning to Dowser she commanded, "Sit. Stay."

She went back into the bedroom for her kit, and when she returned, she found the Doberman and the man watching each other carefully. It was hard to tell which one was more nervous. Biting her lip to keep from giggling, she knelt beside Sam and got antiseptic ointment from the kit.

Sam winced slightly when she applied the cream to the scraped area. "Angel, do you think you could call off the dog? I never did trust big Dobermans."

Ducking her head to hide her amusement, she

said, "He's well trained. He won't bother you unless you make any sudden moves. And my name isn't Angel. It's Max."

"Max? What kind of a name is that for a woman?"

"My full name is Angela Maxwell Strahan. My mother's name was Angela too. I've always been called Max. It saved confusion." She screwed the cap back on the ointment, not bothering to add that her father had told her she wasn't fit to be called by her mother's name.

"Tell me, Angela Maxwell Strahan, what are you doing in Buck and Honey Bear's house?"

"I'm working on a project for Mr. Barton. I'd planned to camp out but he wouldn't hear of it." Max taped a couple of gauze pads over the abrasion and replaced the supplies in the kit. "Hell, lil' lady," she said, tucking her chin and giving a perfect imitation of Buck Barton's gravelly bass, "ain't no sense in that. We've got a weekend place on the river up there sittin' empty as a church on Monday morning. We won't be usin' it for a spell. Honey Bear's draggin' me off to New York City to get some new duds and to go to some of them high-priced art stores." Max smiled at the memory of the gruff old wildcatter who was one of the richest men in Houston. "He said to make myself 'to home.' "

Sam laughed. "That sounds like Buck all right."

Sitting back on her heels, Max looked up at Sam. "Now you know what *I'm* doing here. What are *you* doing here? And why were you trying to break in?"

"I wasn't breaking in."

She cocked an eyebrow. "Funny, you could have fooled me. Most people use doors."

Glancing back and forth from the dog to Max, Sam said, "The Bartons' housekeeper in Houston told me today when I called that my aunt and uncle were in New York for a few days. I was headed for my place down the road, and when I saw the lights on here, I thought maybe some kids were taking advantage of an empty house to have a party. They've been known to do that sometimes. I knocked on the damned door for five minutes and nobody answered."

"Oh," Max said, feeling foolish. "I thought you were a tree limb."

"A tree limb?"

"Yes, a tree limb. Banging against the house in the wind. I told Dowser that's what it was."

"Dowser?"

She nodded toward the Doberman, still sitting where she had commanded, his shoulders quivering as he eyed the man in the chair.

Sam squirmed. "Has he had his dinner? He looks hungry to me."

She suppressed a smile. "He's been fed." Then taking pity on them both, she rose and commanded, "Dowser, heel." Both of the two big males seemed relieved when she closed Dowser in the bedroom, but she felt uncomfortable being alone with Sam Garrett. Even with her back to him, she could feel his green-eyed gaze on her.

And she'd noticed that his eyes were an unusual green, as green as the junipers that clung to the rocky hillsides. No, they were more like translucent jade, more the color of the Guadalupe when sunlight shimmered on its surface.

Turning to face him, she discovered she was right. He was gazing at her as if her robe were invisible, as if those Guadalupe green eyes were magnets pulling her toward him. For a moment she could only stand and stare, as mesmerized by the flesh and blood man in the chair as she had been by the monster on the television screen. She could feel the same kind of reactions: a flutter in her stomach, a prickling of her skin, a pulsing in her neck. Somehow he frightened her, which was strange. Men had never frightened Max, only monsters. And Sam Garrett was no monster—he was all man.

After she had stood there staring for what seemed like an eternity, she cleared her throat and glanced anxiously around the room. "Would you like something to drink?" Why had she asked him that? She didn't want him to stay. She wanted him to go. He made her nervous.

"I'd like that," he said, his deep voice a rumbling caress. "I don't think Honey Bear would mind if we raided her brandy."

When he smiled, a slow, lopsided lift of his lips that crinkled his eyes and deepened the grooves bracketing his mouth, Max felt as if she might dissolve into a puddle on the braided rug. Her fingers fidgeted in the pockets of the plaid robe. She cleared her throat again. "I'll fix it," she said, and hurried to the bar beside the huge stone fireplace that stretched across one end of the room.

Sam sucked in a ragged breath and, with his elbow propped against the chair arm, dropped his head into his hand. His fingers massaged his damp forehead. Godamighty, he was sweating. He'd never had a woman affect him so. Those black eyes of hers had about burned him to a crisp. He'd wanted to grab her and kiss those full pink lips and touch her all over. Angela Maxwell Strahan was some kind of woman: full of spit and vinegar and sexy as hell. He had a feeling she'd tackle a tiger and come out with him by the tail.

Yet, for all her gutsiness, there was something else he saw behind those dark eyes. Maybe it was just nervousness. She didn't know him from Adam, and he *had* tried to break in the house, had nearly scared the pants off her. Recalling their earlier exchange, he grinned. Yes, she was some kind of woman. And he wanted to see more of her—again. He groaned when he remembered the soft curves visible beneath her thin nightshirt.

"Are you in pain?"

He looked up to see Max standing beside him, frowning. "Just a little," he said, feeling a twinge of guilt for the lie. His leg was the furthest thing from his mind. Reaching for the snifter she offered, he gave a blatantly theatrical sigh and said, "I may have to stay here overnight so you can nurse me."

She rolled her eyes. "Come off it, Garrett." Sure, the project was vital to her, but she'd be damned if she'd play games with this overgrown redhead to keep it—no matter how attracted she was to him. Sinking into the sofa that matched the chair he was sprawled in, she tucked her legs under her. "You've probably been hurt worse playing football lots of times."

"Why do you think I played football?"

"Because you're as big as the side of a house. Didn't you play football?"

He shook his head. "Do I look crazy? I'm a gentle kind of guy; I didn't want to get my brains mashed out. I played a little baseball in high school and college."

"And what do you do now?"

"Nothing."

"*Nothing?*"

"Absolutely nothing." He took a sip of brandy and rested the snifter on his stomach. Looking a bit smug, he added, "As of today, I'm retired."

"Retired? Aren't you too young to retire?"

"Nope. Too old. I'd planned to retire by the time I was thirty-five. I missed it by a year."

His comments infuriated Max. Here was this big brute, obviously from a wealthy family, and he could retire. Here she was, she who had worked her buns off for everything she had, struggling to survive. Dammit, life wasn't fair.

"I suppose now you can spend your time sitting on the front porch rocking and whittling," she said, doing nothing to hide the caustic bite of her disdain.

"Now there's an idea," Sam said, nodding, ignoring her sarcasm. "I may even learn to chew tobacco and spit." Then he grinned. "Actually, I plan to do some fishing, some more building around my place, raise a few sheep, maybe some chickens. And I intend to devote a lot of time to painting. It's something I've always wanted time for. The scenery around here is perfect for it."

Max regretted her snide remarks. After all, her troubles weren't Sam's fault. "Sounds nice." Her finger absently traced the rim of her snifter. "So you're an artist."

He shrugged, then abruptly changed the direction of their conversation. "What kind of project are you doing for Buck?"

She reached for her purse on the coffee table, pulled out a business card, and handed it to him. She didn't mention that the ink was barely dry and the cards weren't paid for yet. "I'm the owner of the Never Miss Drilling Company. I'm here to locate water on Mr. Barton's hilltop south of Kerrville and drill a well for Mrs. Barton."

Sam let out a whoop of laughter and Max glared at him. "What's so damned funny?" she asked, grinding her teeth to keep from kicking his good leg.

"Sweetheart, you don't look like any water well driller I've ever seen. And in any case, there's no water on that property Honey Bear wants to build a house on. I know. As a favor to my uncle, I had my best drilling crew sink seven or eight holes up there. If there was any good water to be found, they'd have found it. It's nothing but a pile of rocks with a pretty view. Don't waste your time and Buck's money."

"Do you have a drilling company?"

"No, until today I had a heavy construction company—airports, football stadiums, that kind of thing. But we always had to drill wells to provide our own source of water for construction. My crew was headed by a top-notch man. If he said there was no water, there was no water."

A terrible sinking feeling crawled in the pit of her stomach. Sam must have been the nephew who, as Buck said, "drilled a bunch of doodlebug holes that were drier than a liar's lips." She wouldn't allow herself to believe that there was no water on the hill. There *had* to be. Buck Barton had a hunch there was. He hadn't made millions as an oil wildcatter without good hunches. She had to believe him. She needed that seventy-five thousand dollars.

"I'm a geologist. And a damned good one," she said. "Don't worry about Buck's money. Our deal is: If I don't hit, he doesn't pay. If there's water to be found, I'll find it." Plunking her glass down, she stood and glared at Sam Garrett. "Now get yourself and your . . . leg out of here. I've got to go to bed. *Some* of us have to work for a living!"

Two

Elbows to her sides, Max clutched the prongs of a forked willow branch, holding them tightly in her upturned fists. Watching the skyward-pointed tip for any movement, she slowly picked a path over the rough ground. Despite her thick-soled field boots, the jagged rocks and gravel made her search tedious.

With the sleeve of her chambray shirt, she mopped the sweat off her face and made her way over the rocky terrain toward where her pack lay. It was already one-thirty and she'd barely made a dent in the area to be covered. So far there wasn't a hint of water on the property. Not once had the small limb twisted in her hands, nor had the tip dipped downward. Whistling for Dowser, she sat down on the limestone boulder and laid the willow branch she'd cut this morning beside her. Maybe her skills were just rusty. After all, she hadn't witched for water since she was thirteen or fourteen and under Gramps's careful eye.

When Dowser came bounding up, she scratched

his head and laughed. "You're not having any luck either, are you, boy? I doubt if we're going to find any oil around here." She dug a bowl from her pack and poured him a drink of water from her canteen. As she watched him lap up the water, she sighed. "I wish you were as good at locating water as you are oil. Water," she said, wiggling her fingers in his bowl. "We need to find water."

Dowser sat back on his haunches and gave her a tongue-lolling grin. She tossed him a dog biscuit and watched him trot off to the shade of a scrub oak nearby. Until the bottom had fallen out of the domestic oil market and she'd lost her job with Tex-Ram Petroleum two years ago, they'd made a darned good team. When her witching rod and Dowser's nose agreed, there was always a good producing well drilled on the spot. Nobody ever knew her secret—not even John Ramsey, the owner of Tex-Ram. Everyone simply thought she was an excellent geologist. And lucky, for even the best geologists hit dry holes. Max never did.

For the three years she had worked for him, John Ramsey had rewarded her well. After her first big strike, he'd given her the Ram Charger; after the second, a new Trans Am; after the third, a trip to Hawaii. Then cash bonuses added up to provide a down payment on a house, furniture. The last year John had started giving her a share of the business with every strike. He'd laughingly said that at the rate she was going, it wouldn't be long before she owned more than he did. But with the downswing in the oil business, Tex-Ram went the way of most of the small producers. Oh, they had managed to hold on longer than some, but in the end, the company had folded. Even the big concerns had huge layoffs. And geologists were a dime a dozen.

Max walked to the truck, took a bologna sandwich and an apple from the cooler, and returned to the boulder. A breeze ruffled the damp tendrils around her face and rustled through the scrub oaks as she ate her meal and looked out over the rolling hills, remembering happier times. Remembering summers long ago when she walked those rocky hills with her grandfather.

Sam Garrett paused as he climbed to the crest and watched Max, half reclining and propped on one arm, staring into the distance, nibbling an apple. Even in field boots and blue jeans, she was lovely. All night and all morning his mind had been full of her. Those black eyes had haunted him. He'd half convinced himself that his fantasies had exaggerated her appeal.

He was wrong.

Her hair, in a thick braid over one shoulder, was the same color as the long silky tufts of delicate grass dried golden by long days in the summer sun. The curve of her hip and long line of her leg were a contrast in softness against the weathered gray boulder. He ached to capture her beauty on canvas—or better yet, in his arms.

A crunch of gravel brought Max out of her reverie. Glancing toward the sound, she saw Sam Garrett, thumbs hooked in the pockets of low-slung jeans, sauntering toward her. A deep rust-colored knit shirt, nearly the same shade as his hair, molded his big frame and matched his cowboy boots. A peculiar feeling fluttered over her as she watched his approach. He was even better-looking in daylight.

"Hello," he said, flashing a wide grin. "Found any water yet?"

An answering smile sprang unbidden to her lips. "Not yet. I'm just getting acquainted with the land. It's a beautiful view, isn't it? I can understand why Mrs. Barton wants a house here."

Sam sat down on the hard outcropping beside her and followed her gaze out over the slopes and arroyos where twisted junipers, prickly pear cacti, and stunted mountain laurels clung to the craggy inclines. "It's even prettier in spring." He pointed toward the highway and the open fields below. "When the bluebonnets bloom, that whole area is a sea of blue. Honey Bear loves bluebonnets."

Max laughed. "From the number of paintings at the cottage, I kind of figured that."

"You should see the house in Houston. Her bluebonnet paintings are liberally sprinkled among the Renoirs and the Wyeths. Even I have several. Everyone in the family gets a bluebonnet painting for Christmas. They're real gifts of love."

"She sounds delightful," Max said, tossing her apple core toward a stand of scrub oak where she'd seen a white-tailed doe earlier that morning. "She deserves a home here where she can enjoy the hills. I've always loved this country. In another month or so the sumac will begin to turn red and yellow and orange. My grandfather always said sumac looked like fires dotting the hillsides."

"Your grandfather?"

She nodded. "He lived here until his arthritis forced him to sell his business and move to East Texas with his sister. He had a water drilling company in Kerrville. I spent every summer with him here until I was about fourteen. I adored him. Most of my happiest memories are of the vacations I spent with Gramps. He died less than three years after he left the hills."

"So now you're carrying on the family tradition." Sam picked up the forked branch lying beside Max and began absently snapping off bits of the wood and tossing them toward the spot where Dowser was snoozing. "Are you a ground water geologist?"

Horrified when she noticed that Sam was mutilating her dowsing stick before her eyes, Max almost shouted at him to stop. Then she caught herself and clamped her mouth shut. She couldn't tell him that she was a dowser, a water witch. At best, most people thought that finding water by such methods was superstitious mumbo jumbo. For some reason she didn't think she could tolerate this man, of all people, ridiculing her.

"I beg your pardon?" She'd missed his question when she'd seen him pick up the willow branch. Disgusted with herself that she'd only cut one this morning, she was already figuring how much time she would lose driving to the river, finding another private area with willow trees, and cutting another. A good dowsing stick had to be cut fresh each day, and Sam had destroyed this one.

"I asked if you were a ground water geologist. Is something wrong?"

"No, not a thing," she managed to squeak. "And no, I don't have any sort of hydrogeology specialty. Not in terms of formal training. I've worked mostly in oil. But," she added, challenging him eye to eye, "I have a great deal of practical experience. I assure you that if there's water here, *I'll* find it."

Sam cocked an eyebrow and, with an amused look, gave a little nod as if to concede the point. "How did you and Buck get together? Did you work for him in the oil industry?"

She lifted her chin and announced, "No, I worked for John Ramsey of Tex-Ram. I met Mr. Barton at the Petroleum Club in Houston. He mentioned that he hadn't been able to locate any water here and his wife was heartsick about it. I agreed to take a look."

She didn't tell Sam that she had been working as a cocktail waitress at the posh club that catered to oilmen. She'd figured that, with generous tips, it paid as well as any other work she could find in that economically depressed area. Several of her colleagues with Ph.D.'s were selling shoes or delivering the *Houston Post.* The added advantage of working at the Petroleum Club was that she could pick up rumors there of any kind of an opening for a geologist. She had located a few consulting jobs, but in the last several months there had been nothing.

Desperate, during the summer she'd even tried to sell some of the songs she'd written over the years through an agent in Nashville. A musician friend had recommended the Bullock Agency, but, although Smith Bullock seemed genuinely interested in the tapes she'd sent and agreed to represent her, nothing had come of it. In some ways, that was the most devastating blow of all. It was the loss of a secret dream.

She'd done everything she could to pick up extra money here and there, including several part-time jobs and taking in a roommate to help with the enormous expense of her house. That house she loved so much had taken a healthy chunk of her salary when she'd been riding high, and was now an albatross. It had been up for sale for almost two years without so much as one reasonable offer. If the mortgage company foreclosed, her credit rating would be ruined, and she'd be damned if she would give her father the satisfaction of knowing that she couldn't make it. Not that he'd ever really know—she hadn't seen or talked to him in nine years—but *she'd* know.

With her mouth set in a determined line, she stood and brushed off the seat of her jeans, planning a similar brush-off of Sam Garrett. "If you'll excuse me, I have to get back to my project."

"Great," he said, standing and tossing away the remains of the stick he'd shredded. "I'll tag along and watch."

"Oh, I'm sure you have better things to do than watch me."

He hung his thumbs in the pockets of his jeans, rocked back on his heels, and grinned. "Nope, not a thing."

Max groaned silently. Lord, deliver her from bored buttinskys. Why had she ever thought he was attractive? Right now she'd love to strangle him with rusty barbed wire. The dowsing stick he had destroyed had to be replaced before she could continue her search. Driving back to the river meant at least an hour or two delay. She was losing valuable time. Somehow she had to get rid of him. Politely, if possible.

"It's such a beautiful day," she said, "you should be fishing."

"I've been fishing already. Caught four nice cats. Want to come over for dinner and help me eat them?"

"No, I don't want to come over for dinner. Why don't you go paint some pictures or tend to your goats and chickens and let me get back to work?"

"Sheep."

"Huh?"

"Sheep, not goats. And I have a man who tends the sheep. Anyway, Manuel says there's not much to do with them right now except stand and watch them eat." One eyebrow lifted as he added, "And I'd rather watch you."

"What about the chickens?"

"I don't have any chickens yet. Anyway, I've about decided against raising chickens. They're nasty little things." He hoisted her tool bag. "I'll carry this for you. What do we do first?"

Max rolled her eyes and stomped off. She fought against telling him exactly what he could do as she tried to think of some tactful way, some plausible reason to get him off the site. She had to fetch that willow stick and she didn't relish explaining her water witching methods to Sam.

Hitting upon an idea, she turned and said, "I need to drive into Kerrville and buy some map pencils. I seem to have forgotten to bring mine."

"Great," he said. "I'll go with you. I know just the place to get them. I need some art supplies myself."

"Maybe you should take your own car, then you won't have to make an extra trip."

"No problem. I don't have a car."

She was puzzled. "Then how did you get here?"

"I had the fellow from the station where my

car's being serviced drop me off at the foot of the hill. I wanted to ask you to dinner, and I didn't think you'd mind giving me a ride home."

Three and a half hours later Max was still fuming as they loaded Sam's art supplies in the back of the Charger. He'd practically bought out the store, while she'd purchased a packet of colored pencils she didn't need and couldn't afford. He'd chatted with half a dozen local artists who'd dropped in, laughing and talking to them with enviable ease. And he'd charmed the store owner, a middle-aged lady with a middle-aged spread stuffed into shiny purple stretch pants a size too small.

No doubt about it, Max thought, Sam Garrett had charisma. Lots of it. You could feel it vibrate across the room. It could suck you in if you weren't on your guard—which she was. This russet-haired giant was nothing but a pain in the posterior to her. But somehow Sam had managed to charm everybody in sight—even Dowser, who followed the man's every step, licking his hand and gazing up at him in rapt devotion.

"Benedict Arnold," Max muttered to the Doberman as she motioned the dog up into the truck piled high with easel and palettes and boxes of paints. Dowser didn't even have the good manners to look remorseful.

Any hope of working this afternoon was shot. By the time she delivered Sam and this stuff to his house, cut another willow branch, and drove back up to Honey Bear's hill, it would be almost dark. Damn!

"Nice to meet you," the shop owner said to Max before turning her magenta-painted smile on Sam. Handing him the last of his parcels, she fluttered lashes clumped with black mascara and said, "We'll look forward to seeing you at the Art Association meeting next Wednesday night, Sam."

"I'll be there, Carrie." He hugged Max against him with one long arm and looked down at her as if they were lovers. "We'll both be there, won't we, sweetheart?"

Max wiggled out from under his arm and slammed the back door of the truck. "I'll probably be washing my hair that night." She strode to the driver's side of the Charger and climbed in.

With a smart flip of the wrist, she twisted the key and revved up the engine with an impatient pump of her boot. A swinging Hank Williams, Jr. song blared from the dash radio, and she turned the volume even louder as Sam got in beside her. Almost before he could close the door she spun out with a rubber-laying squeal and roared down the highway toward the little towns of Ingram and Hunt a few miles west of Kerrville. She couldn't shed him fast enough to suit her.

Wide-eyed, Sam looked at her. Turning the music down to a less ear-splitting level, he asked, "Is something wrong?"

"Wrong? You bet your bananas something's wrong. I don't like being used to ward off panting women in purple pants." Giving the knob a defiant twist, she turned the music back up and glared at him.

A slow grin spread over Sam's ruddy face and his eyes took on a devilish gleam. "I believe you're jealous."

"*What!*" she shrieked.

"I believe you're jealous," he yelled over Hank's nasal wail.

"*Jealous*! Why should I be jealous? I hardly know you." This time she turned the volume down, then gripped the wheel as her eyes narrowed. "I'm angry. Furious! I've wasted a whole afternoon listening to you discuss the merits of different paintbrush bristles and watching what's-her-name make goo-goo eyes at you while you grin and lap it up. *I'm* not retired. I can't afford it. *I* have work to do."

Dowser whined and hung his head over the seat to nuzzle his mistress's neck. She patted him and said in a soothing voice, "It's okay. I'm not mad at you, boy. It's okay."

Genuinely contrite, Sam laid his hand on her shoulder. "I'm sorry, Angel. I'll help you tomorrow. We'll get an early start in the morning and make up for lost time."

"No, thanks. I prefer to work alone." *Deliver me*, she thought as she turned up the volume again and tried to ignore the man beside her.

It wasn't easy.

Not even a favorite ballad by Reba McEntire could hold her attention. Energy pulsed from Sam's big frame, filled the cab of the truck, and swirled all around her. His fingers, still resting lightly on her shoulder, seemed to sear through her shirt and heat her skin. His thumb, idly tracing the arm seam, evoked little shivers with every movement. She shrugged his hand away and angled the air-conditioning vent for more cooling.

Why was she reacting to Sam Garrett this way? He was nothing but a pest. She refused to allow herself to think of him in any other way. It irritated her that something in her wanted to wiggle and purr when he came close. What nonsense. She turned the radio louder.

"You must like country music," Sam shouted.

She nodded with a curt dip of her chin.

"Me, too," he shouted again, slouching down in the seat and patting his thigh in time with the Oak Ridge Boys.

He cut his eyes over to watch Max, who was concentrating on the road as if she were driving the Indy 500. Damn, she was something else! A fine looking woman with enough fire to keep a man on his toes. He hated vapid females. Max was fascinating, and obviously bright.

No woman had a right to be so damned sexy. Every hormone in his body went berserk when she was within a hundred yards of him. Yet his attraction to her was more than physical. He wanted to know everything about her, learn her secrets. Make her laugh.

She might be just what he'd been looking for. Yep, she might just be it.

In fact, the more he considered it, he was almost sure.

And the timing was perfect.

Noticing the grim determination of her mouth and the flash of her oil-black eyes, amusement made him bite the inside of his cheek. Even though right now she'd rather die than admit it, Sam suspected she felt some attraction to him. The hints of a current were there. It might take some fast stepping, but he had plans for Miss Angela Maxwell Strahan.

And what he wanted, he always got. Sooner or

later. One way or another. He was patient. And he was persistent.

He reached over and turned the radio down. "Turn left at the top of the hill."

Braking the truck, Max made the turn. She drove slowly down the road that wound beside the Guadalupe, then crossed a bridge that spanned a narrow cascade of rushing water. Giant cypress trees, stoic and ageless, stood with gray boulders amid the current. Spreading Spanish oaks formed an enchanted arch across the lane. Max could almost feel the spirits of Indians and wild game from ages past, almost expected a bronze-skinned brave to step from behind a buckeye thicket.

The setting sun spilled gold over the fall grasses and sparked and danced on the rock-strewn rapids. The countryside was so eerily beautiful, her breath knotted in her throat. The air was rife with the strange presence of something she couldn't name, but moved through her in a poignant fluttering. An incorporeal quality hovered like a mist, so strong she wanted to reach out and grab a handful and rub it into her skin.

"It's . . . it's . . ." Her voice was soft, husky, barely a whisper.

Sam smiled. "It is, isn't it?" he answered quietly. "There's my house."

A sprawling stone house on the rise ahead blended so perfectly into its surroundings that Max almost missed it on first glance. She pulled to a stop in front and climbed out, Dowser following close behind her.

Sam watched as she stood on the terrace wall, arms hugged tight, drinking in the view. He recognized her infatuation with the spot; he'd felt the same way when he'd first found the place ten years ago. To this day the land, the river never failed to fill him with awe. He chuckled. Score another point for his side. He and his property were a package deal. And he wanted her looking at him in that same entranced way.

He walked over to her, then stopped, scratched Dowser's head, and made his move while her defenses were down.

"Do you like fried catfish?"

"Love it," she murmured absently, not looking away from the fabulous view.

"Great. I'll tell Loma to get it started."

"Get what started?" Max asked, coming out of her dreamy abstraction. "Who's Loma?"

"Loma's my housekeeper, and I'm going to tell her to start dinner for us."

"I told you I wasn't having dinner with you tonight."

Keeping a perfectly straight, if somewhat hangdog, face, Sam said, "But you said you liked catfish."

"I do, but—"

"I caught two of them just for you. And in honor of your company Loma has already made potato salad and cole slaw. And her hush puppies," he said, feigning a look of rapture, "will melt in your mouth."

It was tempting. Max didn't think she could face another bologna sandwich when she could have catfish. As if on cue, her stomach rumbled.

He cupped his hand to his ear. "Is that a yes?"

She laughed. "I think that's a yes." She looked down at her grimy clothes and dusty boots. "But I'm not dressed for dinner. I'm filthy."

"No problem," he said, shepherding her toward the house before she could change her mind. "You can take a quick shower in one of the guest rooms. Adrienne and Linda usually leave a bunch of stuff here for when they visit. I'm sure you can find something of theirs that will fit."

"Adrienne and Linda?"

"My older sister and her daughter," he explained, holding open the front door.

An open foyer arched into a huge room with a high beamed ceiling and a wall of glass that wrapped around one end of the house. Designed to take full advantage of the view, every point in the semicircle revealed a different scene, each more breathtaking than the last. The remaining walls were cedar and stone and covered with paintings. An enormous round stone fireplace with a hammered copper hood stood in the center of the room, and Indian rugs were scattered across the polished wood floor. The furniture was plush black leather and heavy nubby cotton in earth tones. It was sturdy and comfortable looking, Max thought. Like its owner.

"Sam, your home is beautiful." She ached to explore, but he directed her down the hall.

"I'll take you on a tour later. I'll tell Loma we're here, then see that Dowser gets fed. I need to clean up a little myself after I unload the truck. Take your time." He grinned and added, "As long as you don't take more than forty-five minutes. I'm starved."

Long before her time was up, Max had showered, washed and dried her hair, dressed, and was standing in the central room admiring a Remington which hung near one of Honey Bear's bluebonnet paintings.

She'd had no trouble finding something to wear. There was underwear that fit—the daughter's, she suspected from the cut of it—and a polished cotton shift in an Indian design of turquoise, tobacco brown, and white had practically leaped off the hanger at her. Turquoise leather sandals decorated with silver conchs fit her well enough. She'd found enough makeup in the guest room to make herself presentable, and left her hair down, adding a matching headband to hold it back.

While she waited for Sam, she looked at all the paintings and sculptures. Several western bronzes by artists whose names even she recognized were on pedestals scattered about the room. An impressive art collection, she thought, but she didn't see a single canvas signed Sam Garrett. Maybe he was modest about his work.

Leaning against the arched doorway, Sam watched Max as she studied a Windberg that was one of his favorites. Damned if she wasn't gorgeous! She looked as if she belonged there. His heart began to swell in his chest. And that wasn't the only thing swelling. He didn't see how he could keep his hands off her much longer.

Chuckling to himself over the effect Max had on him, he walked up behind her and laid his hands lightly on her shoulders. "You look like a blond Indian maiden."

Startled, she jerked and spun to face him. Her hand flew to her chest. "You nearly frightened the life out of me. One of my ancestors would have scalped you for sneaking up like that."

"I didn't sneak. You were lost in that painting." Crossing to a bar tucked in a small alcove, he said, "I've wondered where those black eyes and high cheekbones came from. Indian, hmm? Cherokee?"

She laughed and followed him. "Nothing so civilized. My great-great-grandmother was Apache. The strain was fairly diluted by the time it got to me. You should have seen my grandfather. He looked as if he could have posed for the Indian-head nickel."

"The well-digging grandfather?"

She nodded.

Motioning toward the well-stocked bar, Sam asked, "What would you like to drink? Wine?"

"Jack Daniels. Straight up."

His brows shot up and she grinned. "Working with the men in the oil fields, I learned early on you didn't order something prissy like white wine even if you prefer it."

"I have a great Texas Riesling if you'd like to share it. It's from Llano County. I promise," he added in a stage whisper, "I won't think you're a pantywaist if you drink it."

She laughed and accepted a glass.

Max laughed a lot the rest of the evening. Sam Garrett was a charmer, no doubt about it. Everybody seemed to love him. Loma Mendez, a plump little grandmotherly type who was the fantastic cook Sam promised, absolutely glowed around him. It was obvious that the older woman doted on her "*Señor* Sam" and, from the knowing smiles that brightened her face when the housekeeper glanced between Max and her employer, she was delighted that he had brought home "his *señorita*" for her to fuss over as well.

"Sam," Max whispered as Loma bustled off for their dessert, "you need to set her straight. She thinks that you and I . . . that we . . . well, have something going."

That disarming grin of his flashed and he took her hand across the table. His thumb brushed the tops of her knuckles and she felt a shiver all the way up to her earlobes. "Well, don't we?"

"Certainly not." She jerked her hand away and took a quick sip of water.

He looked amused and neatly turned their conversation to other things. She found that she enjoyed being with Sam, watching him gesture with his wonderful broad hands and long fingers as he described something to her. His deep laughter seemed to vibrate inside her, and he had the most disconcerting way of looking at her. His eyes seemed to caress her. He could make her feel as if she were the only person in the world, someone very special. It was a heady feeling. Her defenses were crumbling fast. She'd have to be very cautious that she didn't allow Sam to interfere with her goal, she reminded herself as she walked to the truck after dinner.

Sam insisted that he drive her and Dowser home in the Charger.

"Then how will you get home?" she asked.

"Walk."

"But it's too far."

"By the road, maybe, but the cottage is just across the river. There," he said, pointing downstream to his right. "It's not more than a few hundred yards. There's a narrow spot where rocks make natural stepping stones across the water."

"But it's dark," she argued.

"I'll take a flashlight."

She sighed and gave in. She was fast learning that when Sam Garrett made up his mind about something, he held on like a snapping turtle.

A few minutes later they were at the door of the cottage. Sam insisted that he stay until she'd deposited her dirty clothes and boots inside and turned on a light.

"Might be monsters in there, hiding in the dark," he joked.

Her back stiffened for the space of a heartbeat, then she laughed. "I doubt that very seriously," she said as she switched on a lamp. When she turned, Sam was standing close enough to touch. "Dowser and I thank you for our dinner."

"You're welcome." His voice was low, and the rugged lines of his face softened as he caressed her cheek. "You're very welcome." He bent to brush the gentlest of kisses across her lips, then turned and walked to the door.

For the longest time, Max just stood there savoring the warm glow his touch had kindled. Her fingers traced lips still tingling from the brief contact.

Finally, she shook herself. If she wasn't careful, Sam could be a real complication in her life, a complication she couldn't afford when she was, quite literally, fighting for survival. She was here to locate water for the Bartons. It was critical that she not get sidetracked.

The timing was all wrong.

Right now she needed Sam Garrett like a submarine needed a screen door.

She dressed for bed and, as she always did when she was restless or troubled, took her guitar and went out on the front porch. Sitting on the steps, she began strumming a few chords of a song that had been forming in bits and snatches.

Green. Guadalupe-green.

Three

Just as the sun was beginning to push the gray from the sky, Max opened the cabin door to let Dowser out and found Sam leaning against the porch railing, thumbs hanging as usual from his jeans pockets. It ought to be against the law for anyone to look as good as he did, she thought. Especially at this time of morning.

"What are you doing here at this hour?" she asked, raking tangled hair from her face and squinting through eyes not yet focusing at full capacity.

"Waiting for you. Remember, I told you I'd help to make up for lost time."

She rolled her eyes and groaned. "I haven't even had breakfast yet. Not even a cup of coffee, and I can't function until I've had coffee. Go away."

"No problem," Sam said, stepping into the house uninvited. He held up a foil-wrapped package. "Loma sent along some of her famous cinnamon rolls. They're still warm. And I'll make the coffee . . . while you get dressed." A glint sparked in his eyes, their green more pronounced because he was wearing a dark moss-colored paisley shirt, and a slow grin spread across his face. "Or, on the other hand, you could wait a while to get dressed."

Looking down, Max realized she was wearing only the thin nightshirt again. "Dammit, Sam Garrett," she muttered. Stomping into the bedroom she gave the door another picture-rattling slam.

Max mumbled as she combed and braided her hair and brushed her teeth, grumbled as she dressed, railed as she laced her boots. She took time for a dab of blusher and a dash of lipstick, though for the life of her she couldn't imagine why she had done it. Certainly not for Sam Garrett. It was all well and good to admit that he was a most appealing man, but allowing herself to get all cow-eyed over him wouldn't pay the rent. Right now falling for a red-headed charmer was way down on her list of things to do. Last night was simply a momentary aberration, she convinced herself.

She didn't need him around mucking up her search. Sam was worse than lint on black velvet. Somehow she had to shake him. Time was running out. She needed a full day of concentrated effort with her witching stick.

And she couldn't concentrate on her business when Sam was around. She jacked up her flagging defenses and strode to the kitchen.

Sam was leaning against the counter, a mug of coffee in his hand, Dowser at his feet. On the table was a plate of cinnamon rolls, a big glass of orange juice, and a second mug of coffee. The breakfast sat atop a place mat with a matching linen napkin beside it.

"Good morning, Angel. Ready for breakfast? I would've fixed some eggs, but I couldn't find any in the refrigerator."

"I usually just have oatmeal," she grumbled, sitting when Sam held out the chair at the place he'd prepared. "Cholesterol, you know." After she'd had a few sips of the reviving caffeine, a tantalizing whiff of the rolls made her taste one. It was heaven. She ate a second and reached for the juice, then frowned. "Where did you get the orange juice?"

"Out of the freezer in the garage. I'm sure Honey Bear won't mind."

Max hesitated. She hadn't intended to play Goldilocks and eat the Bartons' food. It was enough that they were allowing her the free use of their weekend home. Oh, well, she reasoned, there was no need in its going to waste. She loved orange juice.

It was like nectar from the gods. She drank the whole big glass and ate a third cinnamon delight while she tried to think of a way to keep Sam off the hill.

"Sam," she began, "I really appreciate your offer to help me today, but I'm sure you have other things to do."

"Nope, not a thing. I'm free all day."

She carried her dishes to the dishwasher and tried another approach. "I find it distracting with someone else around while I'm working. I do better alone."

"I'll be quiet as a mouse. You won't even know I'm there."

An edge of desperation was beginning to creep

in. The man had the sensitivity of a block of granite. Couldn't he take a hint? Max began to assemble her lunch, still trying to find an excuse to lose him.

Taking the bread and a jar of mayonnaise from the refrigerator, she looked for the package of bologna. Where the devil was it? She pulled out all the drawers. Nothing. She knelt on the floor and peered into every corner. It was gone. How could it have disappeared? The only things in the refrigerator had been a pitcher of water, apples, bread, mayonnaise, and bologna.

"Looking for something?" Sam asked.

"Yes," she said, pulling out every drawer to double-check. "My bologna. It's missing."

"Oh, that. I fed it to Dowser for breakfast."

"You did *what*?" She sat back on her heels in front of the cold, empty shelves and her shoulders slumped.

"I fed it to the dog. He seemed to like it."

The idiot had given her lunch and dinner for an entire week to Dowser for breakfast! If she hadn't been so angry she would have cried. For months she'd been juggling bills, selling everything she owned to try to keep up those enormous house payments. The Trans Am had been the first thing to go, and it had kept her afloat for the first year. But now, even with cutting every corner, it had taken her whole salary to pay her gasoline bill and the utilities, or risk having them cut off since they were two months overdue. God forbid that she should get sick; she hadn't had any insurance since January. She couldn't afford it.

Her roommate Beth's rent payments kept her in

bare essentials—like food. Not filet mignon and eggs Benedict. Bologna and oatmeal.

Sometimes her mouth watered for shrimp scampi or veal parmesan. Instead she had spaghetti, or something equally cheap and filling. More often than not lately, she ignored the rumbling in her stomach and portioned out those slices of bologna as if they were gold. The apples she'd bought on sale had been a real luxury. And now this overgrown wart in a Rolex watch had disposed of her food as if it were nothing. Nothing!

How *dare* he?

Her fists curled in fury. She'd once had a fancy watch, too, but she'd hocked it and bought a cheap one to make last December's mortgage payment.

Jumping to her feet, eyes narrowed and adrenaline pumping, she thrust her finger toward the door. "Out! Get out of here right this minute before I strangle you."

Bewildered, Sam stared at her. "What's wrong, Angel? Is it the bologna? I don't think it will hurt him."

"You insensitive clod! You fed Dowser *my* bologna. What gave you the right? He has plenty of dog food in the pantry. Go away," she said, gesturing wildly. "Just go away. Scram. Vamoose. Get lost."

"But, Angel—"

"Go!"

Plopping back down in front of the empty refrigerator, Max dropped her head into her hands. Try as she might, she couldn't keep a few tears from escaping, and the knot in her throat became a strangled sob. She beat against her thighs in frustration. "Go away," she pleaded. "Now!"

Sam hesitated for a moment, then shrugged helplessly, shook his head, and left.

Dowser whined, nudging in close and licking her face. She put her arms around the quivering Doberman, nestled her head next to his, and rocked as she sniffled and whispered, "It's okay, boy. It's okay. I'm all right."

Max was furious with herself, humiliated that she had acted like a hungry wolf snarling over a bone. Since she'd come here, her nerves had been stretched tighter than what's-her-name's purple pants. Why was she, a mature, independent woman, sitting in the middle of the floor crying over a package of lunch meat?

It wasn't the bologna, she knew. She still had a few dollars for food and, if worse came to worse, she could always sell the truck. It was all that the pitiful package of bologna represented. It was a grim reminder of how close she was to the fear that lurked in a far corner of her consciousness, the fear that plagued her in unguarded moments. The fear that she was useless, that she'd never amount to anything, never be able to make it on her own.

No, she refused to believe it. She'd not listen to those old tapes in her head. She was not stupid, not afraid of hard work. She'd make it. Even if life had dealt her a few blows and seemed to be kicking her while she was down, she'd make it.

Strong. Invincible. *She could do anything*, she reaffirmed in a silent litany.

Taking a deep, shuddering breath, she struggled for control of her emotions. Why had she allowed Sam Garrett to get under her skin? Ordinarily, she wasn't the type to lose her temper, to scream and yell like a wild woman. As a kid, she'd had enough of nasty tempered yelling to last for two lifetimes. Oh, she stood up for her rights—she'd had to learn that early to survive—but she rarely lost control. Never became a shrieking, blubbering mass of hysteria. Yet, that's exactly what she'd been.

And Sam Garrett seemed to be the catalyst.

Poor Sam. She hadn't even thanked him for breakfast. Oh, well, tonight she'd call and apologize for her outrageous behavior. He must have thought she'd lost her mind.

She laughed and gave Dowser a pat. "At least I finally found a way to get rid of him." Feeling strangely buoyant after the spectacle she'd made of herself, she rose and blew her nose on a paper towel. Maybe she'd just needed a good cry to relieve the tension. She certainly felt better.

Keep on peddlin', honey. You can make it. She could hear the words of her grandfather echo in her head. *Don't let the bastards get you down.*

Taking a deep breath, she thrust out her chin and said, "Come on, fellow. We've got to cut some dowsing sticks so I can find Honey Bear's water and save the family homestead."

All the way home, Sam tried to figure out what had set Max off. He hadn't wanted to leave her like that, but she didn't seem to be in any mood to talk rationally. For the life of him, he couldn't make sense of it. Maybe it was that time of the month. Growing up with two sisters, he was no stranger to such things.

But he wouldn't have imagined Max was the type to succumb to hysteria over a package of bologna. She couldn't have cared so much that he'd fed it to the Doberman. She doted on that dog. Why, last night he'd watched her slip pieces of apple pie and cheese under the table to him. It had to be something more. You'd have thought that those few slices of meat were all that was standing between her and starvation.

Sam started at the thought.

No, that couldn't be it. Still . . .

He decided that he needed to make a few phone calls to some friends in Houston. It wouldn't be difficult to do a little checking into Max's background.

By noon, Max's earlier good spirits were beginning to droop. Not once had the willow branch twisted in her fists as she trudged over the rocky hillside. The only water around here seemed to be in her canteen. No, it was too soon to give up; there was a lot of territory yet to cover. From her investigation of the area ground water maps, she knew that the best chance to find water would be in veins, the most difficult kind to locate.

"Let's have lunch," she said to Dowser. "Such as it is." An apple and a mayonnaise sandwich didn't sound very exciting.

Stepping from behind a clump of scrub oak and heading toward the truck, Max was surprised to find Sam spreading a blue tablecloth on the boulder where she'd had her lunch yesterday. Before he could see her, she tossed her willow branch behind a bush.

As she approached, he looked up. "Oh, there you are," he said, smiling as if she'd never pulled her screaming demon act earlier this morning. "I was about to come looking for you. Loma fixed us a picnic."

"Sam, you didn't have to do this. I feel terrible about the way I carried on this morning. I don't know what got into me. Things have been crazy lately. It's been tough."

"Want to talk about it?"

She shook her head.

"Are you sure? I've got a good ear, and we all need a little help now and then."

Pride raised her chin. "It's nothing I can't handle, but thanks for the offer."

"No problem." He took her by the shoulders and sat her down on the outcropping, then began to unload a wicker basket. With a paper plate in one hand, his other executed an exaggerated flourish over the bounty spread before them. "I have here some home-fried chicken. Do you prefer light meat or dark?" When she replied that she liked light, he forked two big pieces on her plate. From a thermos he spooned a chilled pasta salad and added crisp carrot and celery sticks that had been packed in ice water. From another thermos, he poured each of them a glass of milk.

"Milk?" Max asked.

"It's good for you. Calcium and stuff. Don't you watch the commercials?"

After he'd tucked a napkin under her chin and filled his own plate, Sam sat down and looked at Max. His face was beaming with a smile that spread almost the width of his broad square jaw. Like an open-faced little boy, he looked proud enough of himself to pop his buttons. "Now I ask you, isn't this better than bologna?"

Max couldn't keep a straight face. Her smile matched his. At that moment she had the greatest desire to hug him as if he were a cuddly puppy. "Infinitely," she answered, and bit into a piece of chicken.

Why, she asked herself, did Sam have to be so darned nice? She certainly didn't deserve it. Anybody else would have been long gone after the fool she'd made of herself this morning. And why did she have an almost overwhelming urge to sit in his lap and have him hold her?

She found herself staring at his forearms, watching the muscles flex as he ate a piece of chicken, watching the play of sunlight over the red-gold hair dusted along their length. Then his arms stilled and she glanced up. He was gazing at her in the strangest way. It was an odd combination of tenderness and something else she couldn't quite define. But the look was so potent, it took two swallows for the bite of pasta to get past the stricture in her throat. She turned away and forced her attention on her food.

Soon their meal was finished. Max rose to help put away the things, but Sam stopped her. "I'll take care of this," he said. "Are you sure you don't want a brownie?"

She patted her stomach. "I can't eat another bite. I'll save mine for a snack this afternoon. I need to get back to work. Thanks for lunch. And thank Loma for me."

He stood with his hands on his hips, smiling as she walked away. She turned and waved. "Thanks again." He returned her wave, still standing there.

Wasn't he going to leave? she wondered. She ducked behind a thick juniper, parted the branches, and peered through the opening. The basket was packed, but Sam wasn't going anywhere. In fact he was retrieving something from behind those trees.

An easel. A folding stool. A case. Dear Lord, he was going to stay right there and paint. She groaned. Sam Garrett *was* like lint, exactly like lint. For a while she'd simply have to search areas that were out of his sight.

Sighing in exasperation, she retrieved her dowsing stick from behind the bush and trudged off over the rocks.

Several times during the next hour or two, Max almost tripped and fell flat on her face. Visions of broad shoulders, broad chests, broad smiles, auburn hair, and magical green eyes kept flashing into her mind and she would stumble. At the oddest moments, niggling memories of a tingling soft kiss crept into her head and her toe would stub an unseen rock the size of a bowling ball.

Sam Garrett was playing havoc with her concentration. Lecturing herself about safety and attention, Max forced her mind to stay on the business at hand before she sprained an ankle or worse. She must have heard that lecture twenty times before she called a halt.

By midafternoon, she'd found no promise of a vein, so she stashed her willow branch and headed back toward the truck. Sam was, of course, still sitting at his easel with Dowser dozing at his feet. She'd peeked through the juniper branches several times during the afternoon, hoping he had left. No such luck. She had a feeling about an area that she wanted to try, but it was in his range of vision. Lord, what a mess. And it was all Sam's fault.

Well, Mr. Garrett would just have to move his butt off this hill. Enough was enough. She was damned tired of sneaking around like a philandering deacon. One way or another, she was going to get rid of him. Now. Time was running out.

With one brush between his teeth and another in his hand, Sam was frowning at the canvas. When he heard the crunch of gravel under Max's feet, he took the brush from his mouth and smiled.

Max felt her heart turn over. It was hard to stay irritated with a man who smiled like that. It was a struggle to remain resolute in her aim when her fingers ached to tangle themselves in the russet wave falling across his brow.

There. She'd admitted it. She wasn't any more immune to Sam's charm than anyone else. The cold truth was she was tempted to kiss him rather than send him away. But she was going to send him away. She had to.

"Hi," he said when she drew close. "Ready for your brownie?"

"Hardly." She laughed. "I'm still stuffed from lunch." Curious, she peeked over his shoulder at the canvas he'd been working on so diligently.

"What do you think?" he asked.

Cocking her head first to the right, then to the left, Max squinted at the blobs and streaks of gray and green and blue. The painting didn't look like anything she recognized. Six-year-olds could do better. Maybe he was one of those impressionistic artists. She never could make heads or tails of their stuff. Discreetly clearing her throat, she moved back a step and squinted again. It was terrible.

"Interesting," she said, nodding sagely.

"I'm not too happy with it. It doesn't look like I want it to."

"How long have you been painting, Sam?"

He glanced at his watch. "About an hour and forty-five minutes."

"No, I mean how long . . . ever?"

A hint of amusement played at the corner of his lips. "About an hour and forty-five minutes."

She clamped her teeth together and held her breath to keep from laughing. "This is your first?"

He nodded. "Pretty awful, huh?"

"Well," she said, trying to spare his feelings, "maybe awful is too strong a word."

"Look at it from down here." He pulled her into his lap. "It's awful."

"Perhaps you need to take a few lessons to learn the basic techniques."

"I think you're right." He wrapped his arms around her and rested his chin atop her head. "It's damned frustrating. I can see the scene so clearly in my mind. I wanted to paint you lying on that boulder over there. Beautiful, soft, the way you were when I came upon you eating the apple yesterday. In my mind I paint like Andrew Wyeth."

A painful ache of tenderness filled Max's chest and she turned to face him. Her fingers stroked the frown lines away from his forehead, then trailed along his temple to caress his cheek. "Someday you will."

She could see the hunger, the longing in his gaze as she looked at him. At first she thought it was his desire to paint. Then she realized it was for her. It was her face, her form she saw mirrored in the depths of Guadalupe green. And her image was filled with the same longing. At that moment water wells were the farthest thing from her mind.

"Angel," he whispered. "My Angel."

His lips lowered to hers, first brushing gently, the tip of his tongue played across the slight opening of her mouth. His touch was as soft as the breeze ruffling the sumac, as warm as the sun on her back. Then with a groan, he deepened the kiss, clutched her tighter to his chest, and plunged his tongue between her lips.

Caught up in delicious sensation, Max matched his fervor, whimpering as she ran her hands over his muscled shoulders, threaded her fingers through the thick auburn hair.

One large hand slid up her rib cage and cupped her full breast. His thumb slowly stroked her nipple, and when she strained toward his palm, low growls vibrated deep in his throat as his tongue thrust deeper.

Dear heaven, she thought. She was going to die from the longing swelling within her, from the hunger tearing at its leash. It was terrifying. It was wonderful. She held him tight, losing herself in the protective intimacy of his arms as her spirit soared over the hillsides.

Never had anything felt so marvelous, so right.

When at last they broke apart, they were both breathing hard. Sam leaned his forehead against hers and said, "Lady, you're something else."

She gave a throaty little laugh and blew out a soundless whistle. "Fellow, you're something else yourself. My toes may never uncurl."

He threw back his head and gave a lusty laugh of delight. "Angel, we're going to make a hell of a team."

She snuggled in the nest of his strong arms, listened to the sound of his heartbeat against her face, and savored the words.

"Are you through for the day?" he asked, his voice low and suggestive.

Through? Lord, thanks to Sam, she'd barely started. When her hormones settled down and her good sense reappeared, Max was disgusted with herself that she'd let things go so far. She closed her eyes and took a deep breath. She didn't have to be a genius to figure out what Sam had in mind. And she'd encouraged it. What in the world had she been thinking?

That was the problem. She hadn't been thinking. She'd simply plastered herself on him like a price tag from a discount store. She'd intended to send Sam home, or somewhere, anywhere, so she could witch this area. What had happened to her good intentions? She didn't have to be a genius to figure out that one either.

Some way she had to convince him to leave. She *had* to find that water. And soon.

She withdrew from the comfort of his lap and stood. "I'd like to check one or two more things." She took another deep breath and said, "Sam, go away. I have important work to do here."

"But, Angel—"

"Sam," she said firmly, narrowing her eyes and planting her fists on her hips, "go home and watch your sheep or go sign up for painting lessons or go bug what's-her-name at the art store, but stop bugging me. Please."

He grinned. "Have I been bugging you?" He reached and pulled her back onto his lap.

She shoved him away and scrambled to her

feet. "Dammit, Sam Garrett, you are without a doubt the most thick-headed male God ever put on this earth." She looked around for his car. "How did you get here today? Did you plan for me to drive you home again? If you did, get in the truck. The sooner I get rid of you, the sooner I can get some work done."

He stood and motioned over his shoulder with his thumb. "My car's parked at the foot of the hill. I didn't want to drag the bottom out of it on this rough road. Looks like I'm going to have to buy myself something more serviceable if I keep coming up here."

Deliver me, Max thought, rolling her eyes heavenward. She grabbed the canvas and the easel and said, "Here, let me help you carry your stuff down."

By the time she reached the foot of the hill, Max was breathing hard, partly from having almost run the entire way, partly from sheer exasperation. Sam, carrying the rest of the things, was close behind her.

When she saw the big Jaguar parked beside the road, something about that maroon pile of money with leather seats sparked a renewed irritation in her and her lip curled. "That yours?"

He nodded and opened the trunk.

"Very fancy. What do you put in the radiator? Perrier?"

He laughed. "Now there's an idea." He took the canvas and easel from her and stowed the things away. "Thanks for helping, Angel." Leaning down, he dropped a kiss on her nose. "I'll pick you up for dinner about seven."

She scowled. "I'm not going out to dinner with you."

"Want me to come back up on the hill and help you some more?"

"But . . . but," she sputtered, "that's blackmail."

He shrugged.

She glared.

"Seven," he said.

Max muttered all the way back up the hill. Sam Garrett had a way of making her talk to herself. Maybe she was going crazy.

An hour later, she was still muttering as she tramped over the rocky terrain, a fork of the willow branch in each fist. The tip of the limb pointed skyward, mute, mocking. She trudged onward through the rough gravel, more determined than ever to find a vein of water.

The little quiver in her hands was so faint she almost missed it.

Max stopped, her heart pounding. Not a dip, but definitely a quiver. She moved on and the branch stilled. Moving over a few feet, she walked a path parallel to the one she'd just completed. Another quiver.

Excitement began bubbling like a spring deep inside her. But she mustn't get her hopes up yet. It was just a quiver, a hint of the possibility. It might be the edge of a big vein or it might be nothing of any consequence. She laid down her forked stick on the spot, then retrieved her rock hammer, several spads, and some red plastic ribbons from her tool bag. She hammered a marker into the rock where she'd felt the first quiver, another into the second.

After a few more passes, she had put down

three more markers. They formed a meandering path toward the big gray boulder where she and Sam had picnicked.

Moving in a zigzag pattern with the dowsing rod held firmly in her hands, she slowly snaked her way toward the huge outcropping suspended at the edge of the crest. Her boots slipped and slid on the uneven, rock-strewn ground.

The quiver of the branch grew to a shimmy. The shimmy became a shake.

Vibrations from the rod were soon like powerful spasms that shook her arms and shoulders. Slowly the agitated limb began to turn in her hands. Hardly able to contain her mounting excitement, Max fought to keep the tip upright, but the willow bark twisted off in her fists as the branch writhed like something alive and the tip convulsed downward.

She let out a whoop as she dropped the branch and flung her arms in the air. "Hot dog, there's water here! I knew it. I knew it. I knew it!"

Dowser barked and came running to where she was laughing and dancing around on the edge of the steep incline. Tears mingled with laughter as she jumped up and down, squealing with joy. "Water! I found it! I found it!"

Dowser's whole rear end was wiggling as he joined in the game, barking and leaping up to lick his mistress's face. Suddenly, Max was thrown back as the big Doberman made an exuberant lunge, and the loose rock gave way under her foot.

Arms flailing in a desperate attempt to grab something to break her fall, she tumbled down the craggy slope.

Jagged rocks and thorny growth ripped at her clothes and skin as she slid. Frantic, she clutched and clawed, trying to seize a handhold. Her arm hooked around something and she grabbed it with her left hand. A scream of pain tore from her throat as the sharp spines of a prickly pear cactus sank into the soft flesh of her palm.

She held on.

For a moment she lay still, face down in the dusty gravel, fighting the nausea flooding over her in waves. When she had battled it down, she looked around her, assessing her predicament. A scrub oak grew from a crevice only inches from her right hand. She reached for it, and when she held a thick branch firmly in her grasp, she let go of the cactus. Looking up, she saw that, even though it had seemed like miles, she'd only fallen a few feet. Dowser stood on the gray boulder whimpering, staring down at her.

"I'm okay, boy. I'm okay." She hardly recognized the shaky croak that came from her throat. Moving her arms and legs, she decided that nothing was broken. Just scratched and scraped. And her hand was full of cactus spines.

Beyond the stunted oak, the incline was less steep. Using the limbs of the tree, she carefully made her way a few feet across the pitted hillside until she could climb to the top.

Cradling her left hand against her body, she patted Dowser who stood waiting, quivering like a willow branch. She couldn't scold him; she was quivering just as badly.

After a few deep breaths, she examined her hand. Scraped and swollen, it was full of cactus spines. And it hurt like hell.

She swiped at her dirty, sweaty face with her torn sleeve. Her dowsing was over for the day at least. She'd have to wait until tomorrow to confirm her finding and estimate depth. Knees trembling, she walked over to her toolbag and picked up a ribboned spad. Awkwardly using one hand and her feet, she drove the marker into the final spot.

When she stepped back to watch the red plastic ribbon flutter in the breeze, she managed a feeble smile.

"I found it, Sam," she whispered. "By damn, I found it."

Four

Still riding an adrenaline high over her find, Max headed back to the cottage. Even with her excitement to buoy her, driving was awkward and difficult. Her throbbing hand, full of cactus spines, was practically useless, and something crept into her mind, bringing more discomfort.

Why had her first thoughts been of Sam when she'd marked the vein? She didn't need to prove anything to him.

Don't kid yourself, she argued. Sam's opinion of her mattered. She wanted him to think she was special, needed his approval, ached to see pride in her shining from his eyes. Now that her financial solvency was on the horizon, she allowed herself to consider the possibility of a relationship with him. She liked the idea. He had his faults, of course—stubbornness headed the list—but she had to admit she was enormously attracted to him. She'd never met anyone who affected her quite the way Sam did. Every time they were together he snuggled in a little closer to her heart. He could stir all kinds of emotions with just a smile.

And his touch. Well . . .

When her stomach gave a flutter of anticipation, she realized she was actually looking forward to seeing Sam tonight. Mentally searching her limited wardrobe for something to wear, something sexy and feminine, another snippet of an elusive tune flitted through her thoughts and she hummed as more words formed in her mind.

Green, green, Guadalupe-green. It's the color of your eyes.

Sitting on a kitchen stool and leaning over the sink, Max was still humming as she picked the last of the stickers out and poured peroxide over her swollen hand. It had taken nearly an hour to do the job, first using tweezers, then a needle. Dowser had lain at her feet the whole time, looking remorseful and whining each time she unconsciously winced.

"Don't take it so hard, fellow," she said, scratching his head as she moved to the refrigerator to get some ice. "I know it was an accident. You were excited, too."

She opened the freezer compartment and frowned. The space was full of frozen dinners, the expensive kind. Where had those things come from? She could have sworn that it had been empty before. Puzzled, she opened the refrigerator door.

The racks and drawers, which had been almost bare this morning, were laden with food. Jugs of milk and orange juice. Two cartons of eggs. Bacon and chicken and steaks and lamb chops. What looked like a bushel of fresh fruits and vegetables filled every other available spot.

And on the bottom shelf, with a big red bow around it, lay a huge roll of bologna. It must have weighed ten pounds.

At another time and another place, the gesture might have been endearing. Or at least funny. But Max's sense of humor had deserted her. She knew this was Sam's doing. And he had hit her most vulnerable spot: her pride. She was heart-sick. She was embarrassed.

She was livid!

He might as well have taken out an ad in the newspaper announcing: *Poor little Max Strahan can't make it on her own.* It was as if he'd patted her on the head like a child and said, "Let the big man take care of you, honey."

"Damn you, Sam Garrett! Damn you! I don't have to take your charity."

Heedless of her injured hand or Dowser cowering under the kitchen table, she grabbed a plastic garbage bag from the pantry and began to stuff food into it. She didn't miss a single lamb chop or frozen dinner. Every lettuce leaf and every grape was tossed in. When it was full, she twisted the bag shut and glared at it, trying to decide what to do with it. She considered several alternatives, including hauling it over to Sam's and dropping it down his chimney, as well as a few anatomically impossible, but devilishly tempting, options.

Then an idea hit her and she glanced at her watch. Sam would be here in less than an hour expecting to take her to dinner. Mr. Garrett would have a surprise waiting.

She dragged the heavy sack to the front porch

and left it there. She propped the roll of bologna beside it and pinned a note to the red ribbon telling him exactly what he could do with it.

After flipping on the porch light, turning the lock, and securing the safety bolt, she slumped against the front door. She felt absolutely exhausted. Drained. Her boots seemed like concrete blocks. Every prick in her palm and fingers, every scratch and scrape on her body screamed at her. She looked down at her filthy clothes in disgust and sighed. Pushing herself away from the door, she started for the bathroom, stripping as she went.

A shampoo and a shower washed the grime away. Then Max drew a steaming tub of water, dumped in a box of Epsom salts, and sank into its warmth to soothe her aches. But the bath couldn't reach the worst ache. It was the one that squeezed her heart and yearned for what might have been.

Something interrupted the peaceful fog enveloping her. Max started and sat up, splashing tepid water onto the floor. She must have fallen asleep. A loud banging noise was mixed with Dowser's whining and scratching at the bathroom door. She climbed out of the tub, quickly dried off, and wrapped a towel around her.

"Sam Garrett, no doubt," she said, giving Dowser a comforting pat on her way to the living room. "Who is it?" she yelled at the front door.

"Who in the hell do you think it is?" a deep voice yelled back. "Let me in!"

"Go away!"

"I'm not going anywhere until you open this door and talk to me."

"You're going to have a long wait, Mr. Garrett."

"Dammit, Max, open the door!" The doorknob rattled and the banging started again.

Max hitched up her towel and glared at the door. "If you don't stop that and go away, I'm going to call the police."

The pounding stopped and Max waited, straining her ear against the door, listening. After a few minutes, she relaxed. He must have given up. She tiptoed to the living room window and eased the curtain aside to peer through the slit. His car was still there.

"Are you going to tell me what this is all about?" a voice behind her asked.

She nearly lost her towel when she spun around. Sam stood not five feet away, hands on his hips. Even in the dim lamplight of the room, she could see his jaw was clenched, his eyes narrowed.

"How'd you get in here?"

"Through the bedroom window. You really ought to keep it locked, you know. The burglar's still at large."

"I like the fresh air, but you can be assured that I'll lock it just as soon as you leave." She lifted her chin and tried to look as haughty as possible, given that her only attire was the precarious blue towel she clutched over her breasts.

Sam's languid gaze traveled the length of her, and she was keenly aware that she was naked under her skimpy covering. She wanted to dash for the nearest closet, but she'd be damned if she'd give him the satisfaction of knowing she was uncomfortable.

"I thought we had a date," he said, affecting a bewildered expression, one of such wide-eyed innocence that she had to stifle the urge to throw a lamp at him.

"That was before Lord Bountiful snuck over here and filled the refrigerator with his largesse. I don't need your charity. I think my note made it quite clear what you could do with your bologna."

Uh-oh. He'd done it now, Sam thought. Troubled over what he'd found out about Max's financial situation, he'd been so pleased with himself when he'd come up with the idea. Hell, he couldn't let her starve. But he hadn't counted on her fierce pride. Most women he knew would be delighted to take what he offered, but he was fast discovering that Max was not like most women. He'd miscalculated, and now she was madder than a scalded cat. It would take some tricky maneuvering to get out of this one.

He fought back a smile. She looked so damned cute standing there fighting with that towel, damp hair curling around her freshly-scrubbed face. It took every ounce of his willpower to keep from taking her in his arms and loving her until some time next week. Lord, he wanted her.

Careful of every word, he said, "Angel, I don't know what you're talking about. Why would you think I'm offering you charity?" She opened her mouth to speak, then clamped it shut. He shrugged and went on, "I thought you might be tired after working on that hill all day, so I figured maybe we could cook dinner here tonight, have a casual evening at home rather than going out."

He could see her shoulders relax a bit, and he plunged on with his explanation. "I went to the grocery store to pick up some steaks and potatoes, and some stuff for a salad. Then I decided you might rather have chicken or something else, and every aisle I went down, I thought, 'She might like this.' And before I knew it, I had a basket full. Then I figured maybe we could have the rest tomorrow night."

Max eyed him with suspicion. Was he telling the truth, or was this a first class snow job? "What about the bologna?"

"I thought you'd get a kick out of it." He grinned. "Would you rather have had roses?"

It was the grin that did it. She felt its warmth slide over her like a down comforter. Even her bare feet tingled. An answering smile spread across her face, and she shook her head. "You'd probably have bought the florist's whole supply."

"Probably." He ventured close enough to touch the face that was becoming so dear to him.

Their eyes met and held as his finger traced the contour of her cheek, trailed to her chin to rub the slight indentation there, slipped along her neck to her shoulder. A sense of shivering delight rippled over her, and she moved her head to one side and arched her neck like a kitten begging to be stroked. His finger continued its meandering path over the curve of her shoulder, then paused.

He frowned and looked down at a spot his finger skimmed. "What's this?" he asked, indicating the scrape on her shoulder.

"I had a little accident today after you left. It's nothing serious."

"What kind of accident? Where else are you hurt? Did you see a doctor?"

He began examining every exposed inch of her,

and if she hadn't clamped down on the towel with her elbows, she suspected he'd have jerked it away and examined the rest of her.

"Sam!" she said, twisting away. "I didn't need to see a doctor. I told you it wasn't serious. I fell and got a couple of scratches and a few cactus needles in my hand."

"Where? Let me see." He grabbed both of her wrists and turned her hands palm up. "My God, Angel," he said, wincing as he gently touched the injured hand. "Are they all out? Are you in pain?"

Max was finally able to assure him that she wasn't a candidate for intensive care, but he insisted that she rest while he prepared dinner. He practically pushed her into the bedroom.

"While I think you look lovely in a bath towel, Angel, I believe I'd concentrate better if you'd put on something a little less . . . distracting."

She dressed in a well-worn sweat suit, its navy color muted by repeated washings, and slippers. Her hair was difficult to manage with her puffy fingers, so she gave it a few swipes with the brush and tied it back with a red bandanna. She added a touch of makeup to her face and frowned into the mirror. Not exactly the sexy image for tonight that she'd planned earlier.

When she walked into the kitchen a few minutes later, Sam was stowing the last of the groceries back in the refrigerator. He'd shed his jacket and the sleeves of his blue shirt were rolled up.

"Looks like we lost a few eggs, but everything else seems intact," he said. "You sit down right here," he added, steering her to the kitchen table and seating her. "And put your feet up on this." He dragged a second chair over and stretched her legs out on the cushioned seat. "I've made an ice pack for your hand."

Uncomfortable with his ministrations, Max squirmed. She wasn't used to anyone taking care of her. She'd been on her own since she'd been old enough to tie her shoes. "Sam, I don't need an ice pack."

"Sure you do," he said, taking her wrist firmly and wrapping a kitchen towel filled with ice cubes around her hand. He laid her arm on the table, then poured a glass of wine for her. "Now you sip this while I rustle up some dinner." He tucked another towel into his waistband and opened the refrigerator. Frowning at the contents, he asked, "Steak okay? Or would you rather have something else?"

"Steak's fine."

He took out a package of rib eyes and studied the gas stove for a moment. He stared at the dials and opened the oven door, then closed it and looked perplexed.

Max bit her lip to keep from smiling. "The broiler's on the bottom."

"I knew that." He retrieved the broiler pan from the lower compartment and arranged the huge steaks on it. "I've got everything under control. You just relax and drink your wine. How's that ice pack feel?" When she assured him that it felt all right, he whistled as he liberally salted and peppered the meat, then, with a great flourish, sprinkled on half a bottle of garlic powder he found in the spice rack.

Max almost choked on her wine, but she didn't say a word. It seemed that Sam did everything in a big way.

After he'd managed to start the steaks broiling, he picked up two potatoes and looked from the stove to the objects in his hands, then back again. "Uh," he said, nonchalantly glancing toward Max, "how long do you like your potatoes baked?"

"Usually about an hour," she replied, struggling to keep the laughter from her voice. When he looked stricken, she added, "If I'm in a hurry, I use the microwave."

A look of relief came over his face, and he nodded. "Me too." He thrust the potatoes into the microwave and fiddled with the timer for a moment. That done, he took a sip of his own wine and gave her a self-satisfied grin. "Now for the salad."

Gathering vegetables from the crisper, he tossed them in the sink and rinsed them, then began chopping with a vengeance.

Max sniffed, then sniffed again. "Sam?"

He stopped his assault on a stalk of celery and turned to her. "Yes, Angel?"

"I think the steaks are burning."

He yanked open the broiler and flames shot up a foot above the charred meat. As he doused the fire with a glass of water, a loud explosion came from the microwave. He strode over to it and jerked open the door. He stared at the mess in the microwave, then turned to Max. "I think we lost one."

She couldn't contain herself any longer. She hooted with laughter.

In the end, Sam called the local barbecue joint and paid a kid twenty dollars to deliver dinner. With it they ate the salad he'd made. When Max complimented him on it, he managed a sheepish grin. "I do salads best," he said.

After they were finished, he poured them each another glass of wine and began stacking their dishes in the dishwasher. He'd cleaned up the earlier mess while they waited for the delivery. Even Dowser had turned up his nose at the blackened, garlic-laden remains of his efforts at broiling steaks, and, while the Doberman munched on dry dog food, the meat had gone down the disposal.

Sam had handled the whole fiasco with such good humor that Max couldn't help but be touched. She watched him as he moved about the kitchen, remarkably graceful for a man of his size. She liked the bigness of him: the breadth of his shoulders, the strong thighs evident under the lightweight slacks he wore. Everything about him spoke of strength and confidence, yet he was sensitive and gentle as well. It had been obvious that he was no cook—his culinary skills were only slightly better than his artistic ones—but he'd plunged right in, willing to give it a try. She wondered what kind of lover he'd be. Bold, she suspected. Imaginative. Adjectives flitted through her mind until she barely could catch her breath.

Sam turned to look at her just as she licked her lips. He leaned back against the counter, feet crossed, unruly shock of russet hair across his forehead, dish towel still tucked into his waistband. He lifted his wineglass and drank from it, watching her over the rim.

The kitchen was filled with sexual awareness.

It bounced off the ceiling, pulsated from every corner. It was so potent Max couldn't breathe at all. She couldn't move. Her heart felt like a rock hammer beating against her ribs.

The telephone rang. They didn't move. It rang again.

On the third ring, Sam muttered an oath and snatched up the receiver from the wall behind him. "Hello." The greeting was an impatient bark. His scowl softened and he said, "Oh, hello, Uncle Buck. It's Sam." After a pause he said, "Having dinner." He looked over at Max and winked. "Yes, she is. But you'd better watch out, you old lecher, or I'll tell Honey Bear on you." He laughed at something his uncle said, then held out the phone to Max. "He wants to talk with you."

She rose, her muscles beginning to stiffen up from her spill, and, trying not to limp, stepped to the phone. "Hello, Mr. Barton. This is Max Strahan. I may have some good news for you."

"You mean you think there's water on that hill, little lady?"

"I'm pretty sure."

"Hot damn! Honey Bear's gonna be whoopin' and hollerin'. I had a hunch about you, gal."

Max laughed. "I need to do some more testing tomorrow, but if things are as I suspect, we'll start drilling in a few days. You'd better get your checkbook ready."

"Hot damn! I may give you a bonus. Honey Bear's gonna keep me up all night, she's gonna be so tickled. We'll be back in Houston by the end of next week. If you hit it before then, give us a call up here at the Plaza Hotel in New York City."

Max took down the number of their hotel suite and said her good-bye. Buck Barton's excitement had been infectious. After talking to him, her previous exhilaration over the project had returned. Still grinning, she turned to Sam. A deep furrow creased his forehead.

"You didn't tell me you'd located a drilling site today," he said.

"You didn't ask. And anyway, as I told Mr. Barton, I have to do some more testing before I'm sure of the best spot. I can't afford to drill any dry holes."

Sam chewed on the inside of his lip, trying to decide what to say. She looked so happy and excited after talking to Buck. He didn't want to burst her bubble or hurt her feelings, nor did he want to make her mad again. But he knew there wasn't any water on that hill. He took her injured hand in his, looked at it carefully, then dropped a feather-light kiss on her palm. The swelling was down some, but it was far from healed. And although she'd tried to hide it, he'd seen her limp. It wrenched his gut to think that she'd be scrambling around on that rough ground trying to find something that wasn't there.

"Angel," he finally said, "you're in no shape to work tomorrow."

"I have to, Sam. I have no choice. Anyway, I'll be fine by morning."

"Why is finding water on Honey Bear's hill so important to you?"

She hesitated for a moment, then looked into his worried eyes. "I need the money."

He almost breathed an audible sigh of relief. She'd finally admitted to him that she had a problem. "Oh, hell, sweetheart, if you need money, I'll loan—"

"No, Sam. Thanks for offering, but I don't want

your money. I can handle this by myself. Mr. Barton will pay me when I bring in the well."

Sam hugged her to him and nuzzled his face in her sweet-smelling hair. What was it about this black-eyed angel that made him want to coddle her, protect her, shield her from disappointment? He drew back and scanned her face. "Are you so sure there's water there?"

"I'm positive."

She said it with such fervor that she almost convinced him. "Then go for it, Angel. I'm with you all the way." Hell, if it took drilling a hole to make her happy, he'd help her sink holes all over the damned hill.

Max felt as if she were drowning in green, so powerful was the spell of Sam's gaze. His head lowered and his lips met hers in a moist kiss. With a soft sigh, she melted in his arms, savoring the breathless wonder of the taste of him as his tongue nudged past her parted lips.

She reveled in the power of the strong arms around her, delighted in the heartbeat pounding his chest against her hand. She clung to him as his tongue thrust against hers and he pulled her closer to his body.

His fingers slipped under her shirt and kneaded the bare skin of her back. There was longing in his touch, yet she could feel him holding back. Demanding, she ground her pelvis against his and whimpered.

Sam went wild. Growling deep in his throat, he pulled her hips against him. When she sucked in a cry of pain, he went dead still, then dropped his hands and broke away.

"Oh, Lord, I hurt you. I'm sorry." His breathing

was ragged and his expression alarmed as he looked into her face.

She smiled and smoothed the lines from his brow. "You didn't really hurt me, Sam. I think you just located another bruise from my fall."

He dropped a quick kiss on her lips. "I'd better go and let you get some rest."

When she walked him to the door, he reminded her to lock the bedroom window. "I've been wondering," she said, "how you got in to leave the groceries."

"Buck and Honey Bear left a key with Loma in case of emergencies. But I promise," he said, smiling down at her, "I won't use it again without your permission. Unless it's an emergency."

She grinned. "Whose definition of emergency? Yours or mine?"

He laughed and kissed her nose. "Good night, Angel."

Max found herself humming again as she locked the door and the window. More words for the song came.

I chase my haunted dreams . . . with green, Guadalupe-green . . . cries.

Five

The first golden rays of the sun were breaking over the hills as Max pulled the truck to a stop and got out. She turned up the collar of her windbreaker against the slight chill of a northerly breeze, stuck her fingers in the back pockets of her jeans, and breathed in the fresh, clean air of the hillsides. Yawning, she stretched to loosen the kinks before she began her search. How she would have loved to be snug in bed right now, catching a few more hours of sleep.

It had taken a long time for her to fall asleep the night before. Of course the thrill of her find had kept her adrenaline pumping, but it was more than that. Every time she closed her eyes, memories of her evening with Sam replayed in her mind: his laughter, his touch, his kiss. The very scent of him lingered in her nostrils. She must have dozed and awakened half a dozen times until she finally decided to get up. Well before dawn she had loaded her gear in the Charger and whistled for Dowser.

Her early start was partly excitement and partly

a need to leave before Sam could arrive and put a crimp in her plans. As fond of him as she was growing, he always seemed to divert her attention from everything else.

Even now, when she needed to be about her business, she was thinking about Sam. He had been so sweet last night, treating her like a princess on a pillow. She was surprised that someone so obviously masculine could be so sensitive, so solicitous. That side of him didn't fit the image of the typical corporate executive. Oh, there was no doubt that he was used to bossing people around. She'd seen that side of him too. And she'd gotten the full force of his overprotective streak. Although she had to admit that she'd enjoyed his fussing, she didn't need his clucking over her like a broody hen today, of all days. First things first, she reminded herself once more.

After flexing her hand a few times she decided that, while it still felt a bit tight, the pain was gone and she could use it well enough to work. The few sore spots from her fall barely registered as she studied the serpentine row of markers. In the light wind of early morning, red ribbons flirted along the rocky ground, teasing, enticing her to test the spot again.

A rush of anticipation made her laugh and punch the air with a short jab. By damn, she'd found it! She'd have the money in hand before the week was out. Almost giddy, she did a little shuffle and reached into the truck for a forked willow branch.

To validate her discovery, she searched the area anew, pacing paths across the line of markers. Each time, the dowsing rod dipped the same as it had yesterday. Starting at the outer perimeter, she followed the trail of spads toward the large boulder. As she neared, the quivering of the branch became more pronounced. She fought to keep the tip turned upward, but again the bark skinned away in her hands as it writhed in the throe of a downward spasm.

"What in the devil are you doing?"

Max's head shot up. Dressed in old cutoffs and a faded orange sweatshirt, Sam Garrett stood almost close enough to touch. She looked from him to the branch in her hands, then back to Sam again. When she released her hold on one fork, the rod stilled, but she felt her stomach turn over and a terrible sinking feeling spread through her. She couldn't bear for him, of all people, to ridicule her, and she searched her brain for some plausible explanation, or even a glib lie, but her mind was as blank as a new blackboard. There was nothing to do but brazen it out.

Lifting her chin, she said, "I'm locating the best place to drill for water." She looked him straight in the eye, daring him to laugh. "What are you doing here?"

His eyebrows were drawn together and his expression was solemn. "I somehow knew you'd be back on this hill at first light. How's your hand?"

"My hand is fine. I'm a fast healer."

He looked at the row of spads and plastic ribbons. "What are those?"

She glanced over her shoulder at the trail he indicated. "Markers."

"What kind of markers?"

He wasn't going to leave it alone, she thought, and sighed. "They indicate the path of a water vein," she replied, trying to be as noncommittal as possible.

Cocking his head, he gave a little nod as if to say, "I see," when it was obvious he didn't see at all. "How could you tell where to mark?"

She closed her eyes and took a deep breath. Her shoulders slumped in resignation. Again her gaze met his and she held up the willow branch. "With this."

"With a stick?" He seemed puzzled for a moment, then his expression changed slowly as he grasped what she was saying. "Do you mean you're a water witch? I thought you were a geologist."

"I *am* a geologist," she said. "And I'm not any kind of a witch. I'm a dowser."

For Sam to say he was shocked would be an understatement. He couldn't believe that Max would be involved in such superstitious nonsense. Surely she didn't expect to drill a well based on some kind of hocus-pocus. The whole idea was outrageous. Crazy. He was just about to voice his opinion when he noted the pugnacious tilt of her chin. He was beginning to recognize that unconscious gesture of hers. Nobody had ever accused Sam Garrett of being a fool. He wasn't about to do or say anything to get her dander up again.

"Hmm," he said, struggling to keep his comments neutral and his thoughts to himself. "Interesting. How long have you been doing this kind of thing?"

"Since I was a little girl. My grandfather was a dowser." She searched Sam's face for any sign of censure but found none. Breathing a small sigh of relief, she relaxed. "I know you probably think it's crazy—most people do, so I usually don't talk about it—but I'm really quite good at it." She laid the branch on the boulder, wiped her damp hands on her jeans, and leaned against the big rock.

Sam picked up the forked stick and examined it. "Why don't you show me how this thing works."

So used to keeping her special talent a secret, Max hesitated for a moment, watching him closely for any expression indicating his interest wasn't genuine. He seemed sincere. And he hadn't laughed outright. For that alone she wanted to hug him.

"Okay." She picked up the rod and walked to a place away from the markers. "I hold one prong in each hand with the tip pointed up like this." She demonstrated the correct position, then added, "Now I walk slowly across an area." She stepped a few paces. "If there's no water, nothing happens. But watch what happens when I approach the spot I've marked." As she came closer to her prime target, the branch began to quiver violently, then turned down again. "See?"

"Well, I'll be damned." Sam shook his head. "I've never seen anything like it. Here," he said, reaching for the rod, "let me try that."

Walking slowly over the rocky terrain, he imitated Max's action. Nothing happened. Not a single wiggle or a quiver. He tried again. Nothing. "It doesn't seem to work for me. Are you sure it isn't your imagination?"

Indignant, she shot him a black glare. "Of course it isn't my imagination! I've been dowsing for water and oil for years. I've *never* missed. Ask John Ramsey how many dry wells he ever hit where I told him to drill."

"My God, woman, do you mean to tell me that a company actually hired a dowser to find oil?"

Oh shoot, she hadn't meant to tell him that. Feeling uncomfortable about her disclosure, she mumbled something and shrugged.

"What?" he demanded.

Scowling, she repeated, "I said they didn't exactly know how Dowser and I located it."

Sam glanced over at the Doberman who sat on his haunches, lolling his tongue and looking from Max to Sam. "Do you mean he's in on it too?"

"He doesn't seem to be any good with water, but he's great with oil."

"Does he have his own little stick?"

"Dammit, Sam, you don't have to act like such a horse's rear about it!" She turned and clomped off toward the truck.

He caught up with her and grabbed her by the shoulders. "Angel, I'm sorry. But this whole thing has taken me by surprise. You have to admit it sounds peculiar. Why don't we have a cup of coffee and you can explain to me how it works."

He picked up a thermos leaning against a tree, poured two mugs full, and handed her one.

"Where did this come from?" she asked.

"I brought it for you to wake up with this morning, but you were gone when I got to the cottage." He took a sip from his cup and said, "Explain about the dowsing."

"Nobody seems to know exactly how it works. I've done some reading about it. Although a lot of scientists in the United States think it's a bunch of bunk, a few of them have been investigating the phenomenon. And the Russians have been studying it seriously for years. Certain individuals seem to have the ability to locate subterranean deposits—everything from water to all kinds of ores. The art of radiesthesia, or sensitivity to radiations, has been practiced for at least seven thousand years. Did you know that engineers in Vietnam used dowsing rods to find tunnels and booby traps?"

"I'm intrigued," he said. "But why does it work for you and not for me?"

She shrugged. "I don't know why it works for some people and not for others. My grandfather said I had 'the touch,' but I suspect it's simply something we don't understand yet, some biophysical sensitivity that acts according to perfectly natural laws, like a dog's keen sense of hearing or smell. Dowser can sniff oil and I can find it with a rod. We always agreed and we always found oil."

"You mean that dog can sniff oil?"

She nodded. "But I suspect that it's because of where I found him. I was working in the oil patch when I came upon him. He was little more than a puppy, beaten and half starved. Somebody had treated him badly and he was almost dead. I took him home with me and nursed him. I've always supposed he associates my finding him with oil, because he can sniff it out."

She took a swallow of coffee and watched Sam, who seemed to be deep in thought. She wondered if he believed a word of what she'd told him. And she wondered if his feelings for her would change now that he knew about her strange ability. Suddenly, that thought brought a profound ache to her throat and a hollow feeling to her chest. It was as if the world were on hold while she waited for his reaction.

Finally he looked up and smiled. "Well, Angel, if

you're convinced there's water here, I guess we'd better decide what to do next."

A gush of happiness burst through her and she smiled as the world moved again. He believed her. "There's water here all right. I just have to figure out how deep to drill." She set her cup down and opened the truck door. She selected a straight willow stick about a foot and a half long and walked back to the site with Sam trailing along behind.

Max squatted down beside the boulder and held out the stick a few inches above the last marker and parallel to the ground. It began bobbing up and down rapidly, and she felt a jolt of excitement as she watched it.

It was exceptional. Shallow and at least thirty gallons a minute.

"Look at it, Sam. Look at it!" She jumped up and threw her arms around him. "Did you see that? Did you see it? Oh, I can't believe it." She was laughing and crying and kissing him. "Oh, Sam, isn't it wonderful?"

He caught her to him. "I like it," he said, grinning as she planted more kisses on his face. "I think you missed a spot right here." He pointed to his chin. She laughed and smacked the place he indicated. "Now it's my turn," he said, leaning down to drop a kiss on her chin, another on her cheek. Another on the corner of her mouth.

But his kisses weren't quick busses spawned by an exuberant spirit. They were soft-lipped, slow, and trailing promises of things to come. The mood changed as his tongue traced the outline of her lips, flicked across the slight parting of them. Then his mouth slanted over hers with a hunger that was palpable. Warmth flooded her whole body, and she pulled his head down, straining to increase the delicious sensation.

With one broad hand he scooped her hips closer against him while the other slipped inside her jacket and found her breast. His hand was almost rough with need as he stroked the soft flesh. He rubbed her against his pelvis and she could feel the strength of that need.

Pulling his mouth away, he nuzzled the side of her neck. His breathing was ragged as he said, "Touch me, Angel. I think I'll die if I can't feel your hand on my skin."

A surge of desire poured through her, and she glided a hand up under his sweatshirt, rubbed along his back, slipped around to explore the taut muscles of his chest. She felt him shudder under her fingers, and she grew heady with the knowledge that her touch could affect him so.

"Do you have any idea how much I want you, Angel? I lie awake at night imagining your sweet hands on me, imagining you lying in my bed, imagining my . . ."

His words made her knees go weak, and his lips claimed hers again with a fierceness that brought oblivion to everything except the two of them. His tongue thrust into her mouth with bold rhythmic strokes and he reached for the snap of her jeans.

At the sound of the pop, Sam and Max both stilled. He dragged his mouth from the kiss and leaned his forehead against hers. Both of them were shaking, and her breath wasn't any steadier than his. She was mortified that she had allowed things to go so far with a man she'd only known for three days, that she had been ripe and ready to make passionate love with Sam Garrett on a rocky hill. In broad daylight. In front of God and everybody. It wasn't like her. She didn't *do* things like this. But then she hadn't been herself since the night she'd nailed Sam's pants to the wall and first looked into those green eyes.

What must he think? It was her fervent wish that a fissure would open beneath her feet and she would slip into it and drop to China.

For what seemed like eons to her, Sam just stood there, eyes closed, sucking in great gulps of air. After a while he chuckled.

"Love, you do strange things to my body and my good sense. In another minute I'd have had you stripped and on the rocks." He refastened her jeans, straightened up, and stepped back. "I didn't mean to get so carried away." He ran shaky fingers through his thick auburn hair. "Not with *you*. Not here. Not now."

She looked up at him and blinked. Now she was even more embarrassed. And irritated. Not with *her*, he'd said. A mountain of old insecurities teetered, threatening to crush her. Did he think she was beneath him? She fought the old feelings, stiffened her spine, and glared at him. Wasn't an out of work geologist good enough for a retired millionaire sheep tender cum lousy artist? Well, he could just—

He cupped the side of her face and rubbed a gentle thumb across her lips. "I have other plans for you, Angel. Long-range plans. And softer places in mind for the first time we make love."

As she gazed into river-green eyes filled with tender yearning, with warmth and laughter, Max was mesmerized. Her thoughts fled. She couldn't have strung enough words together to make a coherent sentence if her life were at stake. Compared to Sam, Svengali was a neophyte.

"Right now, my lovely water witch, we need to get this show on the road." He slapped his hands together and rubbed them. "I figure that the sooner we can get somebody up here to start drilling, the sooner we can get on with"—he shot her a licentious grin—"more important things. How deep do you think we'll have to drill? Most wells around here are seven or eight hundred feet. That's as deep as my crew drilled any of the holes. Maybe we can go down to nine hundred or a thousand. It's worth a try."

His words were like a bucket of ice water. The spell broke and her chin came up. "We? *We?* Where did you get this *we*? It's my project, Sam. I can handle it without any help. But thank you for offering," she added stiffly.

"Do you have your own crew and equipment?"

She shook her head. "No, but I'll arrange for it today."

"Sweetheart," he said, draping an arm around her shoulders, "do you know how much per foot it costs to drill through solid rock?"

There was that condescending tone again. It made her hackles rise. "Certainly," she said, shaking off his arm. "I'm not stupid. But *I* won't have to drill a thousand feet. Or even seven hundred. The water is less than a hundred feet down."

"A hundred feet? Hell, Max, nobody hits water around here at a hundred feet."

Her chin lifted even higher and her black eyes narrowed. "Well, *I'm* going to hit water at a hundred feet. Even less than that, I expect. Maybe nearer seventy-five. And furthermore it's going to pump enough to keep Honey Bear's swimming pool, and half the swimming pools in Kerrville," she added, waving her hand toward town, "full to the brim."

With that, she stomped off toward the truck and climbed in. Damn Sam Garrett! With him about, her emotions bounced around like a paddleball. He was making her crazy. She revved the engine a couple of times before she spun out, spewing gravel in her wake. In her rearview mirror she could see Sam standing where she'd left him, hands on his hips, shaking his head and talking to Dowser.

Dowser. Damn. She slammed on the brakes, opened the door, and whistled. The Doberman looked up at Sam, licked his hand, then dashed for the truck.

Well, he'd done it again, Sam thought as he stood on the hill watching Max roar off. He winced when she almost collided with a juniper stump, then breathed relief when she whipped around it. Was he ever going to learn? Every time he tried to help her—and he knew she damned well needed some help—that little chin came up and she got stubborn as a mule and madder than the dickens.

Why was she determined to be so all-fired independent? Why wouldn't she let him do things for her? He could make her life a whole lot easier. He liked doing things for her. Wanted to do things for her. He'd have been willing to hire a drilling crew and let them sink dry holes in this rock from now till kingdom come. He could afford it. She couldn't.

Maybe there was something to this dowsing business, but he didn't think so. He'd had a psychology course or two. He suspected that she wanted so desperately to find water that she'd unconsciously moved her hands and made the branch quiver. Lord, he'd never forget the ecstatic look on her face when that stick bobbed up and down. She was going to be devastated when she didn't find that vein of water at a hundred feet. His gut wrenched at the thought of her being hurt.

Somehow he had to figure out a way to help her. It wasn't going to be easy. He wondered if it was worth it. Then he remembered black eyes that could melt him with one glance, a body that molded perfectly to his, lips that could set him on fire. There was chemistry between them for sure, but there was something more. For all his grumbling, he admired her more than any woman he'd ever met. He was enchanted by her, head over heels about her. Max had a spirit that matched his. They would make a hell of a team. And he knew, if he could tap it, she had a well of love inside her that would never go dry.

But damn her stubborn pride! It was giving him fits. Did he really want Max in his life? Was she worth the aggravation?

Hell, yes.

As Sam started down the hill to his car, he began planning his next move. He'd give her some time to cool off, then come up on her flank.

Max stopped at the Dairy Queen and got curly-topped cones for Dowser and her. Now that she was about to come into money, she could afford the extravagance. She loved ice cream. Somehow it was comforting. After her encounter with Sam, she needed it.

Dowser devoured his in two bites and settled down to snooze in the back of the truck while Max leaned against the door licking hers slowly, savoring the taste on her tongue. She absolutely refused to allow any thought of Sam Garrett to enter her mind. Except that she was going to prove to him that she was right about the water.

After she finished the last of her treat, she wiped her fingers and got a notebook from the glove compartment. There was a phone booth in front of the convenience store next to the drive-in, so she trotted over to it and opened the Yellow Pages. The listing for drilling companies in the area was very small. She copied down the names and addresses and got directions from an old fellow who was collecting aluminum cans from the trash bin beside the store.

The closest one was only a couple of blocks away, so she headed for it first. A bell tinkled over the door as she entered the office. Sitting at a desk was a plump lady wearing lots of rouge, her yellow hair piled into a nest of ringlets atop her head.

"May I help you?" the woman asked, looking up from filing her thumbnail.

"I certainly hope so," Max replied. "I need to hire someone to drill a water well. As soon as possible. Like tomorrow."

"Oh, honey, I'm afraid you're out of luck. Earl's got both his crews on a big job over in San Antonio. The soonest he could get to you would be right after Thanksgiving."

"Well, thanks anyway," Max said, managing a smile.

"Don't mention it. Say, you might try Jesse Sebastian over in Ingram."

Max glanced at her notebook. "He's on my list. I'll drop by there."

"Better yet," the woman said, picking up the phone, "why don't you have a seat and I'll give him a call and see if he can take a job."

"I'd appreciate that." She sat down in a hide-bottomed chair next to the desk. After so many years in the big city, she had forgotten how neighborly people in small towns were.

"Hello, Ruth? This is Mary Lou. Listen, I've got somebody here looking for a driller and you know Earl's over in San Antonio . . . No, you don't mean it. When did that happen?" The woman shook her head and frowned. "Is there anything I can do for you?" She shook her head again. "Well, now you let us know how he gets along, hear?" Mary Lou hung up the receiver and said, "Jesse had a heart attack last night at the supper table. Just up and keeled over in the mashed potatoes. He's in the hospital. It looks like he's going to be all right, but he won't be working for quite a while."

Max must have looked crestfallen because the woman grabbed up the phone again. "Let me try a couple of more people."

There wasn't a single driller in the area who'd be available for the next five or six weeks.

Max began to panic. "I've got to find someone. Maybe I could get a crew from another town. Maybe from Austin or San Antonio."

Mary Lou looked sympathetic. "Honey, I know for a fact that you couldn't get anybody from San Antonio. Every drilling company around there is tied up on the same job Earl's on. And if you hired someone out of Austin, it would cost you an arm and a leg. In advance."

Max swallowed back the bile that was rising in her throat. "How much is an arm and a leg?" When the woman told her, she almost fainted. There was no way on earth she could raise that kind of money. She had planned to pay for the drilling out of her profit. "There's got to be someone who can drill that well for me. I'm desperate." Tears began to gather in her eyes. She was so close. So close. She couldn't lose it all now. This was like somebody's idea of a sick joke. "There has to be someone."

"The only other person I can think of is . . ." Mary Lou twirled a stiff yellow curl around her finger. "No. No, he wouldn't do."

"Who? Have you thought about another driller?" Max felt a glimmer of hope, sat up straight in her chair, and leaned forward.

"Well," Mary Lou said, wrinkling her nose, "I suppose if you're really desperate, you might try Goose Gallagher. But he's over eighty years old, and most of the time he stays drunker than Cooter Brown."

Max slumped back in the chair. It was like an eleventh hour reprieve. "Right now I'd try the devil himself if he had a drilling rig. Let's give him a call."

Goose Gallagher didn't have a telephone, but Mary Lou wrote out the directions and drew her a map.

Max crossed her fingers and said a prayer as she drove down the winding road by the river.

Goose Gallagher's place was little more than a shack. No, it *was* a shack, she revised as she pulled up to the decrepit structure beside the river bank. Put together with mismatched, unpainted boards, it listed north about twenty degrees and looked as if it might collapse at any moment. In the yard, a dilapidated school bus, minus wheels and windows, sat gathering rust under a pecan tree. It looked as if it hadn't run in thirty years. Five or six chickens scratched at the bare ground beside its gaping door. Two goats pulled at the high grass growing between a discarded wringer-type washing machine and a twisted bedspring propped against a pile of rotting lumber.

Max parked behind an ancient pickup held together with baling wire and determination. Ordering Dowser to stay in the Charger, she got out and picked her way through scattered debris and chickens and animal droppings. Beer cans of every imaginable brand littered the area. The old collector at the convenience store could have had a field day here.

Rounding the house, Max stopped and stared. A precarious porch, shored up by stacks of rocks, faced the river and was attached to a rickety pier extending out over the water. On the sagging porch an old man sat in a rocking chair, rocking back and forth and swigging from a can of beer. She felt as if the bottom had dropped out of her stomach, as if her last hope had been snatched away. Mary Lou had said he was over eighty. He looked a hundred.

God only knew when his worn khaki shirt and pants had been washed. He had about a two-week growth of white whiskers, and irregular patches of liver spots stained his bald head, pink and slick as a baby's bottom. His nose was large, hawk-shaped, and covered with a spidery network of red. He must have had a thousand wrinkles around the rheumy blue eyes that looked up as Max approached.

She forced a smile on her face and stepped up on the porch. "Morning," she said. "You must be Mr. Gallagher. I'm Max Strahan." She stuck out her hand.

The old man tossed his beer can onto the pile nearby and rose. A little unsteady on his feet, he wiped his hand on his britches leg and extended it to her. "Most folks just call me Goose. What can I do for you, little lady?"

She was surprised by the strength of his grip. Gnarled and rough with calluses, his was the hand of a working man. And his shoulders, though slightly stooped, were almost as broad as Sam's. "I'm looking for a good water well driller."

"Well, you've come to the best," he said, puffing out his chest, then catching himself on a post as he swayed. "Drag up a chair and let's talk business." He pointed to an aluminum lawn chair leaning against the front wall.

Max unfolded it and sat down carefully, testing her weight against the seat, which had several strips missing. When Goose settled back in his rocker, she told him the location of the well she wanted drilled.

He shook his head. "Little lady, there ain't no

water out there. You'd just be throwin' your money down a rat hole. I've been drillin' around here purt near all my life, and I've run afoul of that place before. You'd have to accidentally hit a vein off the Edwards formation, and they're scarcer than hen's teeth."

Max couldn't believe it. He was turning her down. She had to find some way to convince him. Goose Gallagher was her only chance. "What do you think about dowsing?" she asked, broaching the subject carefully.

"Witching, you mean?" Max nodded. "Well," he said, running his hand over his whiskers, "I know some folks don't hold with it. And me, it never worked for me. Tried it a time or two. There's some around here who think they can do it, but they ain't really no better at findin' water 'n anybody else. Wasn't but one feller I ever saw that could do it. Him and me used to partner some, but he's been gone from here for a lot of years. Heard Dal died."

Her heart almost stopped. "Dal?"

"Dal Maxwell. Damned good witcher. Never saw him miss."

"He was my grandfather, Goose. And I'm just as good as he was."

Max had said the magic words. Soon she and the old man were trading stories about her grandfather, and he agreed to drill the well. The only problem was, as usual, money. It seemed that Goose had tied one on a couple of weeks ago and driven his pickup into the fountain in front of the courthouse. Tom Phillips, the local sheriff, had confiscated his drilling equipment until he paid the damages.

"Didn't hurt my pickup none, but I tore that fancy new fountain all to hell. Tom said the mayor told him it would take about two thousand dollars to fix it back. And I ain't got the wherewithal."

Max almost groaned. Where was she going to get the money? Maybe she could get a loan at a local bank. Promising to get back with him when she raised the cash, Max headed for town.

All the banks were closed. She had forgotten it was Saturday and, by the time she arrived, after noon. Unless she could come up with another idea, there was nothing to do but wait until Monday. As she drove back to the cottage, it occurred to her that she could borrow the money from Sam. She quickly discarded the idea. She'd sell the Charger first—and that was her last resort. It was her only remaining asset of any value. She stroked the leather seat beside her. She'd hate to part with this vehicle; she loved it. It had been her first big bonus, and they had traveled a lot of miles together.

When she pulled in the driveway, she stopped and let Dowser out for a run, then turned toward the house. Waiting on the steps were two huge baskets of red roses. She parked quickly and ran over to the house; she laughed as she read the note.

This is all the florist had.
Love,
Sam

She took the baskets inside and put one arrangement in the living room and the other in the bedroom. Cupping one bud in her hand, she inhaled the sweet fragrance. No one had ever sent her roses before. She was humming as she went in to take a bath, fantasizing all sorts of delicious scenarios for tonight.

"A softer place," he'd said.

It was almost ten o'clock. The chicken was dry, the broccoli was mush, and the parslied potatoes had congealed in their butter. Max stashed the whole mess in the refrigerator and blew out the candle on the table. Where was Sam anyway? She'd been sure he would come over. Now she felt like a fool for putting on a silk dress and sexy underwear. She didn't even know why she'd packed such things.

She tried not to think about Sam, knowing that with the least provocation the lump in her throat would change to tears. Instead she put on a nightshirt, popped a big bowl of popcorn, and climbed into bed to watch *Invasion of the Body Snatchers*.

Her body clammy and tangled in twisted sheets, Max came half awake. Dowser whined and his wet nose nudged against her cheek. The room was dark. Her heart was still pounding heavily with the horror of a nightmare. Monsters, body snatchers, had surrounded the house and were about to come in the windows after her. She'd been trying to scream, but no sound would come from her throat. It had seemed so real.

The Doberman whined again and raised his head toward the window, which was at her back.

Max's heart switched to triple time as childhood

terrors rose up like specters, sucking the air from her lungs, paralyzing her limbs. It *was* real! "They're here," she whispered with lips almost frozen by fear.

Her first inclination was to bury her head under the covers and wait, shivering, for the inevitable. Using every bit of willpower she possessed, she forced herself to roll over and face the dreaded creatures.

Standing outside the window, his grotesque face illuminated by moonlight, was the most hideous monster Max had ever seen or imagined.

Six

Max screamed and bounded from the bed in a mad dash for the kitchen phone, flipping on lights as she went. Sam's number was the first thing she saw on the note board, and she jabbed at the glowing buttons on the dial. He answered on the second ring.

"Sam, call the police! It's the body snatchers! They're after me!" She slammed down the receiver and sank to the floor.

Knees drawn up to her chin, she sat huddled by the kitchen cabinets, shivering, trying to catch her breath. Dowser lay beside her, his head in the crook of her arm, his body shaking as hard as hers.

A few minutes later there was a hammering on the door. She nearly jumped out of her skin.

"Max! Open up!"

Sam. It was Sam. She ran to the front door. Her fingers were trembling so badly that it took her three tries before she could turn the lock and slide the bolt. She flung open the door and threw herself into Sam's arms.

"My God, Angel, you're shaking like a leaf. What's wrong?"

"A monster. He was after me." She buried her face in his bare chest and waved an arm behind her. "I saw him. In there. Looking in the window."

He held her close and made soothing noises. "It's okay, love. I'm here."

A siren came wailing up the drive, then a car door slammed. When Sam tried to move, Max wrapped herself around him with a death grip. "Don't leave me," she whimpered.

"I won't leave you," he said. "I just need to talk to the deputy for a minute. I'll be right back."

He sat her down on the couch. Something tore inside him as he watched her curl into a ball. He was filled with helpless fury at the thing that had caused such terror. The Max he knew wasn't prone to hysteria. He wanted to roar, wanted to pull up trees and beat the ground with them at the idea that someone would put her in such a state.

He strode outside to where Dick Ware stood, shining his flashlight around the house.

"Everything seems okay," the officer said. "But look what I found in the bushes." He held up a woman's stocking. "She probably scared him off, but it was our burglar all right. We'll check the area, but he's probably long gone by now."

Sam could have kicked himself from here to Austin. If he hadn't been playing games, he would have been with her tonight in her bed. Or his. Damn his stupidity! Well, that could be remedied soon enough, he thought as he walked back inside. He was going to gather up Max and the dog and her stuff and take her home with him where she belonged.

He was surprised when she went along with him without much of a fuss. Since Sam had run across the river, barely taking time to call the sheriff's office before pulling on loafers and a pair of jeans as he ran, he was without a car. He found her keys, packed her bags, and loaded everything into the truck. Max, wrapped in a blanket, snuggled beside him as he drove to his house. He could still feel her trembling.

Max nestled closer to Sam, drawing comfort from the strong arm around her. Maybe her monster had turned out to be just a man with pantyhose over his head, but she had never been so terrified in her life. For that one awesome moment, she had come face to face with the embodiment of every bogeyman she had conjured up in her younger years. She felt like an idiot now. Grown women didn't believe in monsters. It had been a burglar, not a body snatcher. Still, old fears died hard. And she didn't think she could have spent the night alone in that house for a million dollars. She shuddered and nuzzled her cheek against Sam's bare shoulder.

"You don't have on a shirt," she said.

He chuckled. "You scared me so badly, I didn't take time to dress. You're lucky I didn't come charging over in my birthday suit."

"Thanks for coming, Sam. After the broccoli went limp, I was afraid I might never see you again."

"The broccoli? What are you talking about?"

"I fixed dinner for you tonight, but you didn't come and it got overcooked waiting."

Sam felt like a first class heel. He squeezed her to him and said, "Angel, I . . . I . . ."

"It's okay. You didn't say anything about dinner. I just assumed . . ." Her finger traced an idle pattern over his chest, and she felt him grow tense. "Did I thank you for the roses? They're beautiful." She bolted upright as they pulled up in front of his house. "Sam, we forgot to bring the roses."

"Don't worry about the flowers tonight. We'll pick them up tomorrow."

Despite her protests, he carried her into the house. She was far from petite, but he carried her as if she weighed nothing. He wasn't even breathing hard as he strode through the front door, which was standing wide open, and down the hallway. He didn't seem to consider taking her to a guest room. He made straight for his king-size bed and laid her on the side where the covers were thrown back and the pillow indented from his head. A brass lamp on one of the bedside tables cast a warm glow over the room. She felt safe here.

He tossed aside the blanket she'd been wrapped in and pulled the sheet up to her chin. "You stay here," he said, "and I'll get Dowser settled and bring in your things."

Face solemn, he stood and stared at her for a moment before he left the room.

Max turned on her side and snuggled against the pillow. It smelled of Sam. A heady mixture of spices, citrus, and musk. Sexy. Masculine. Like Sam.

The big room suited him, she thought as she looked around. Rich, lush carpet was the same russet shade as his hair. A massive dresser and chest of dark wood stood against natural-colored grasscloth walls decorated with more of the western art he loved. Two easy chairs flanked a table by windows which, Max imagined, looked out over the river.

By the bedside phone two books lay open and face down. She picked up one and read the title. *Painting for Beginners.* She smiled. The other was a Stephen King novel. She scanned the dust jacket and shivered. The taste of fear was still too fresh in her mouth.

Tossing the sheet aside, she got out of bed and found the bathroom. Horrified at what she saw in the mirrors that stretched along the six foot marble vanity, she grimaced. She looked worse than the prowler. Using Sam's brush, she restored her hair to some semblance of order. Then she washed her face and gargled with mouthwash she found by the sink, surprised to find her knees were none too steady.

"Max!"

The sudden bellow startled her, and the mouthwash bottle flew from her hand and crashed into the basin. "Damn," she mumbled, grabbing the towel bar with a white-knuckled fist.

Sam jerked open the door. "What happened in here? What are you doing out of bed?"

"I had to go to the bathroom, Sam, and when you yelled, it nearly scared me out of ten years' growth. I dropped a bottle in the sink. Now look at the mess I've made. I'm sorry. I seem to be nothing but trouble for you tonight." She began gathering up pieces of broken glass, but he stopped her.

He took the shards from her hand and tossed them into a wastebasket. "Forget the damned bottle. Are you all right?"

"I'm fine. I guess I'm still a little jumpy. My legs don't seem to want to hold me up."

He lifted her into his arms and carried her back to bed. When she was under the covers and sitting propped against the pillows, he sat down beside her and brushed a long strand of honey-blond hair away from her face. "Sweetheart, what happened tonight to frighten you so badly? It seems strange that the little spitfire who nailed my pants to the wall would fall apart over a prowler."

Trying to collect her thoughts, she licked her lips and fidgeted with a corner of the sheet. "Well," she said, avoiding his eyes, "I suppose it's because I knew you were a man, and I thought he was a body-snatching monster." She glanced up and saw his puzzled look. Trying to keep her reply light, she managed a feeble smile and added, "I'd watched *Invasion of the Body Snatchers* on TV and was having a nightmare. When I woke up and saw the man at the window, I thought he was one of *them*."

Sam chuckled. "*Invasion of the Body Snatchers*? You're going to have to stick to something a little less ghoulish from now on if movies give you nightmares."

"Oh, no," she said. "I watch scary films all the time. It's part of the desensitization process. You know, if you see something often enough you sort of become immune. Like doctors and blood. Only in my case it's creatures from the black lagoon and werewolves. I have teratophobia."

He frowned. "You have *what*?"

"Teratophobia. A fear of monsters. I've had it as long as I can remember. As a little boy, didn't you ever lie in bed at night and imagine that monsters were under your bed or in your closet? Didn't your parents ever tell you that horrible, child-eating bugbears were there waiting to gobble you up if you got out of bed or were bad?"

"Good Lord, no! Who would tell a child such a thing?"

She dropped her gaze to her hands, which were nervously pleating the hem of the sheet. "My father."

"The bastard."

She gave a little mirthless laugh. "He was that."

"And your mother let him get away with it?"

She shook her head. "My mother died when I was about two. I think my father blamed me for it; she was never very well after her pregnancy with me. He adored my mother and my older stepbrother, Carl, but he never liked me very well. Neither did Carl. I suppose I was something of a nuisance." She shrugged and kept pleating and unpleating the sheet. "My earliest memory was of my father scratching the mattress and telling me that 'Bloody Bones' was under my bed and would get me if I didn't go to sleep. I must have been about three. I think he wanted to go out drinking with some of the other roughnecks and my brother wasn't home to baby-sit. His tactics worked so well, he kept it up. For years I used to lie in my bed petrified. Afraid to breathe."

Sam took her in his arms and held her close. "My God, Angel. I can't imagine somebody doing that to you. I could kill him."

Drawing back and cupping his face in her hands, she smiled at him. "Sam, believe me, he isn't worth the trouble. But thank you for caring."

"Oh, I care, sweetheart," he said, taking one hand and dropping a kiss in her palm. "Do you know how much I care?" His eyes met hers and held. His gaze warmed like green crystal reflecting the sun. "I love you, Angela Maxwell Strahan. I think I have from the moment I first saw you."

Emotion filled her heart near to bursting. She stroked his dear face, her fingers moving gently over the slight roughness of his jaw, and managed to whisper, "Oh, Sam." Tears welled up and stung her eyes as she basked in the wonder of it.

"And I've never, *never* wanted anyone the way I want you." He guided her hand over the fine red-gold hair on his chest. "One touch from you and I . . ."

He closed his eyes and sucked in a deep breath as her hand continued its way alone, then was joined by the other. She slowly stroked spirals over his torso, pausing over a mole here, a hard-muscled ridge there. When his eyes opened, and river-green had ebbed away from a center dark and wide with longing.

He reached for the top button of her nightshirt. "I want to see you, touch you, drink my fill of you."

She watched his face as he unfastened the row of buttons and parted the sheer fabric. When he looked at her and licked his lips, a flash of desire leaped from her lower belly, radiating downward to an ache and upward to a shiver that turned her nipples hard.

Sam watched the change in her breasts with a heavy-lidded gaze. "Lord, woman," he said, then groaned as he leaned forward to flick his tongue over the dusky tips.

He laved the underside of one breast and kneaded the fullness of the other. She arched her back, offering herself to his touch, begging for more. One hand covered his at her breast, the other went to the nape of his neck. He circled a nipple with his tongue, then with a deep growl drew it into the wetness of his mouth.

The sound aroused a need in her more primitive and potent than any she'd ever known. It ripped away her restraint, and she went wild—twisting, whimpering, begging.

"Easy, love," Sam said, pulling away. "We've got all night, and I'm going to look at and taste and touch every luscious inch of you." He grinned. "With you responding to me like that, I won't last thirty seconds."

He tossed the covers aside and slipped the nightshirt from her shoulders. It landed on the carpet by the bed. He stood and kicked off his shoes, then turned to look down at her. While he was still dressed in jeans, only a scrap of beige lace and silk shielded her from his scrutiny. Max grew uncomfortable and reached for the light.

"Don't, Angel. I want to see you. You're beautiful, more beautiful than I dreamed. And I've dreamed of you often." His eyes seemed to devour her. "I'm going to paint you like this some day. In our bed with your breasts still wet from my mouth."

Bending over her, he slipped his hands up the length of her legs as if marveling at every curve and dip. They paused at the band of panties riding low on her hips. His thumbs hooked the lace and slowly peeled the delicate fabric back over the route he'd come. Never taking his eyes off her, he flung the beige wisp over his shoulder.

Starting with her toes, he kissed and caressed his way up her body. Max felt as if she were being worshiped on a pagan altar, but by the time he reached her throat, she was a writhing mass of nerve-endings screaming for release from exquisite torment. He lay half covering her, one leg between hers.

"Sam, please," she begged, but his mouth silenced her with a kiss so breathless and urgent, she almost drowned in the white-hot fury of it. She clung to him, her fingers biting into the flesh of his back as his tongue thrust over hers with a rhythm that caused her pelvis to move against the rough material of his jeans in the same tempo. Her small cries were answered by moans from him, and her hand tugged at his waistband.

He stilled her hand and tore his lips from hers. "Wait, love. Are you protected?" She shook her head and he slipped from her side.

When he stripped off his jeans and faced her, her eyes widened and she sucked in her breath. He was magnificent. Covered with a glistening sheen, he was like a copper stallion, his big frame all taut muscle from shoulder to ankle. He was boldly immodest. And shamelessly aroused.

"You like what you see?"

She nodded slowly and a lazy grin spread over his face. He reached into a drawer of the nightstand and withdrew a packet. Her heart pounded and her breathing was shallow as she watched him. Never had she witnessed anything more erotic than his movements as he stood before her and slowly rolled on the sheath.

She held out her arms and the mattress dipped as he knelt between her parted thighs. His hands slipped along the sides of her legs, her hips, her rib cage, and stopped when each was filled with the spill of her breasts. His thumbs teased the nipples, fanning the sparks of her desire. "I'm all yours, Angel. Body and soul and worldly possessions. And now and forever, you're *mine*."

He lifted her hips and took her slowly, watching her face as he slipped inside. She saw the muscles of his jaw twitch and felt the trembling of his thighs and hands as he fought for control. She saw love in his eyes. And at that gentle moment she knew that she loved him more than anything or anybody she'd ever loved before.

"I love you, Sam," she whispered.

His control shattered in an ecstatic grimace and he plunged into her, hard and deep. Their lovemaking changed from gentle to fevered. It was flash and fire. Hunger and desperation. His hands and his mouth were all over her as he thrust in an urgent frenzy. Their breathing became labored and their bodies slick with sweat as they moved together—arching, plunging, writhing, reaching . . . reaching.

Max touched an inner sun that burst into a million prisms of light as she exploded in sensual delight. She cried out and arched against the source of her pleasure. Sam hesitated a second, then thrust a last time and echoed his release.

After a moment, he rolled away and gathered her damp body close to his side, pulling the sheet over them against a sudden chill. "Are you all right, love? I didn't mean to get so rough. But, Lord, I went crazy. I don't seem to have much control around you. Hell, I don't have *any* control."

She brushed away the auburn locks, darkened

and curly with sweat, that clung to his forehead and smiled. "You weren't rough. You were wonderful. I won't break, Sam. Except for my weird notions about things that go bump in the night, I'm pretty tough."

"You're not tough at all, sweetheart," he said, running one big hand along the curve of her hip. "You're soft as silk. And the only thing that goes bump in the night around here is me. Go to sleep, love. I'll fight the monsters tonight."

His gentle stroking soon lulled her, and her lashes fluttered against her cheeks. For a long time Sam held her, savoring his love for her, planning their future, wondering about her past, about the bastard who'd made her childhood hell. He suspected that anyone who would scare a kid with monsters would do worse things.

When he heard scratching and whining outside the door, he sighed and got up, careful not to disturb Max. Dowser was going to damn well have to learn to sleep in the kitchen.

The smell of coffee teased Max awake. A hand was on her breast, a cold nose on her cheek. She blinked a few times to get her bearings. The hand was Sam's; the nose was Dowser's. The Doberman stared at her with large, soulful eyes and she smiled in understanding. Putting a finger to her lips to signal quiet, she began to ease away from Sam's warm body, which rested spoon-fashion behind hers.

Instantly, his grip tightened and one big leg was slung over hers. "Where are you going?" His voice was husky with sleep.

"Dowser needs to go outside."

"You stay here," he said, nuzzling the back of her neck. "I'll do it."

He didn't move except to trail tickling kisses down her spine to her shoulder blades. Dowser whined.

She giggled. "*Sam.*"

"Okay, okay." He dropped a final kiss on her back, climbed out of bed, and grabbed a robe from the closet. "The first thing we're going to have to do, boy," he said to the Doberman as he tied the belt, "is make you one of those doggie doors."

Dowser looked up at him with a pitiful expression and whined again as if to say, "Can we discuss this later?"

Sam laughed and snapped his fingers. "Come on, fellow." At the door he paused and turned to Max. "Hold my place, love. I'll be right back."

Max stretched like a contented cat. She felt wonderful. Sam was a delightful lover, vigorous and considerate. She couldn't imagine anyone pleasing her more. Not that she was all that experienced, she thought as she arose and padded toward the bathroom. There were only two others she could use for comparison. One, she'd been semi-engaged to in college, and the other was a brief and disastrous fling with an engineer. The sex hadn't been all that great. In fact, she'd wondered what all the fuss was about. Now she knew.

Adjusting the knobs on the shower, she stepped under the warm spray and hummed as she lathered her body, noting a new tenderness in a few places. "Green . . . Guadalupe-green . . . eyes," she sang softly in her deep, throaty voice.

The shower door clicked open and there stood Sam, stripped of everything except a grin and the mug he held in his hand.

"I brought your coffee." He stepped into the spray and handed it to her. "Why don't you drink it while I do wonderful things to your body?"

And he did.

"Sam," she squealed, "I'm getting water in my coffee."

He plucked the mug from her hands and set it in a corner of the shower. "There's plenty more," he growled, and went back to what he was doing.

It was a while before she got another cup.

Later, wrapped in towels, they sat in the middle of his bed sipping orange juice and feeding each other warm, sticky cinnamon rolls. "I love these," Max said, licking a dollop of icing from his finger.

"I'll have Loma fix them for you every morning."

She stilled. "Is Loma here? Lord, Sam what must she think? We weren't very quiet in the shower."

"*You* weren't very quiet, you mean," he said, laughing as he stripped her towel away and trickled orange juice in her navel. "I was very quiet." His tongue licked up every drop, and he filled it again.

"*Sam*. I'm mortified. I'll never be able to face her again."

He rested his chin on her abdomen and cut his eyes up at her. They were alive with dancing green devilment. "Don't worry, Angel. Loma doesn't work on Sundays. She just leaves the coffeepot and bun warmer on automatic timers. There was nobody here to hear your lovely little screams but me." He gave a knowing wink and a rakish smile. "And *I* liked it."

"*Sam*," they both said at the same time.

"Well, I did." Laughing, he scooped her up and rolled over on his back, placing her astride of him. "Have I told you this morning how much I love you?"

It was past noon when Sam loaded the big inner tubes in the back of the truck. The day was warm and sunny, perfect for tubing on the Guadalupe, Sam declared. They were both dressed in sneakers and bathing suits—his, a form-fitting dark blue, hers, a red maillot borrowed from his niece's wardrobe. Both wore Sam's T-shirts.

As he hoisted the picnic basket into the Charger, she asked, "Why can't we use the river right here?"

"Too swift and rocky," he replied. He helped her into the cab and drove down the lane from his house. "There's a better place a couple of miles from here. I can't believe you've never been tubing. I thought you said you'd spent summers around here with your grandfather."

"I did. Those were my loveliest memories as a little girl. I adored him, and we had lots of fun fishing and boating and walking in the hills. I used to beg to live with him all the time."

"Why couldn't you?"

"My father wouldn't allow it. Spite, I guess. He and my grandfather hated each other. Too, I suppose my father didn't want to give up the social security payments that came to me after my mother died. She was a nurse."

"He sounds like a real prince. Where is he now?"

"I haven't the foggiest notion. I left home the

day I was eighteen and could take charge of the trust fund my grandfather left me. It was enough to see me through college."

"And you haven't seen your father since then?"

She shook her head. "I sent him an invitation when I graduated with honors from Texas A & M, but I never heard from him."

"What about your stepbrother?"

"I suppose he's still in the Marines. He joined right after he flunked out of college. My father had high hopes that he would become a geologist or an engineer—something higher on the oil patch pecking order than a roughneck like he was—but Carl wasn't much of a student." Max turned on the radio to a country music station and started singing along with Sylvia.

Taking the cue that the subject of her family was exhausted, Sam said, "This truck surely is a handy vehicle to have around here. I may buy something like it."

"I love the Charger." She ran her hand along the dashboard in almost a caress. "I'd hate to part with it. I like it better than the Trans Am I had for a while."

They pulled to a stop beside the river. Soon the two of them were bobbing down shallow rapids on their inner tubes, dodging boulders and paddling when the current calmed. Dowser ran along the bank barking and twisting his bobtailed bottom with excitement.

They made several trips down the river before they called a break for a late afternoon lunch. They sat on a blanket Sam had spread under a buckeye tree and dined on meat loaf sandwiches and beer that tasted like ambrosia to Max.

"Did you have fun?" he asked.

"Lots of fun. Even if my bottom did get a little battered on the rocks." Sam popped the top of another beer and offered it to her. She shook her head. "I couldn't hold another thing." Her fingers gently touched his shin, where the bruises were fading from purple to a yellowish shade and the scrape was new pink skin. "I'm sorry about this."

"I'm not." His eyes lit with an impish grin. "Think what a story we can tell our grandkids."

Smiling wistfully, Max let the comment go by and lay back on the blanket. Sam stretched out on his stomach beside her and tickled her nose with a tiny yellow wild flower he'd plucked. She had never been so contented in her life. At this moment she didn't have a care in the world. It was unbelievable how her life had changed in the last few days. She had a feeling that things were finally turning around for her.

Seven

Max had a splitting headache and her feet hurt. To top it all off, she could feel a run slither up the leg of her last decent pair of nylons. She shucked her navy pin-striped jacket, tossed it on the seat of the truck, and climbed in after it. Crossing her arms over the steering wheel, she rested her head against them and fought the blue devils tormenting her.

When she had started out this morning—some seven and a half hours ago—there had been a spring in her step and hope in her heart. She had wound her hair up in a neat bun, donned her best let's-talk-business suit, and tied a power-red bow at the neck of her white silk blouse. Convinced that she had the world by the tail, when Sam had asked where she was going, she had smiled mysteriously and told him she had a few loose ends to tie up before she started drilling and, no, he couldn't tag along. She'd be back before he knew it.

Hah!

She'd talked to every reputable financial organization in the area and a couple whose reputations were highly questionable. The bottom line was: No loan.

About midafternoon she'd called her roommate, Beth, to ask if, please God, the real estate agent had called with an offer on her house in Houston. No such luck. The house had been shown a few times but there hadn't been so much as a nibble.

Of course she could always ask Sam to co-sign a note with her or borrow the money from him outright, but that was as good as admitting defeat. She didn't need him to bail her out; she would make it on her own. It was a matter of self-respect.

She sucked in a big breath of air and faced the inescapable alternative. The only thing left to do was sell the truck, but she didn't think she could face that today. Besides, it was getting late and, knowing Sam, he would be ready to send out the Mounties to look for her. She would get a fresh start in the morning. One more day wouldn't matter.

Max could almost hear her father laughing at her as she drove to Sam's. She pursed her lips and lifted her chin. She was strong, she reminded herself. She was invincible.

Sam was waiting at the door when she pulled up. "You look tired, sweetheart," he said as she trudged toward him. He gathered her in his arms and pulled her into the foyer. "I missed you today. Did you get all those loose ends tied up?"

"Not quite." She snuggled against his chest and tucked her head under his chin. It felt so good to have him hold her. Right now his arms were a safe haven in an alien world. She had an almost overwhelming urge to pour out all her troubles, but she resisted the temptation. For all sorts of complex reasons, some she understood and some she didn't, it was important that she wage this battle alone. Instead she said, "I have a few more things to do before we can begin drilling, but somebody's playing a bongo in my skull and these shoes are slow torture. I think I have a blister on my toe."

"We can handle that." He bent down and, with her holding his shoulders for support, took off the pumps and tossed them aside. "Yep," he said, holding her foot on his knee and examining it. "Looks like a blister all right. And you've got a runner," he added, smiling as he slowly traced its path with his finger, "all the way up your leg." His finger disappeared under her skirt.

"Tell me about it." She gave a disgusted snort.

"Bad day, huh?"

"The pits."

"Anything I can do to help?"

She shook her head.

"How about a glass of wine and a bubble bath? My sister Adrienne always said a long soak in a mountain of foam puts the world in perspective."

She managed a forlorn smile. "It couldn't hurt." As they walked down the hall, arms around each other's waists, she asked, "Where's Dowser?"

"He's out playing with Bess and deviling the sheep."

"Bess?"

"She's Manuel's border collie. I think old Dowser is smitten. He may change from oil sniffing to sheep tending."

For the first time that day, Max laughed.

Sam was the dearest, sweetest man, she thought as she watched him fill the sunken tub. Bubbles, as frothy as whipped cream and smelling faintly of lilacs, mounded over the marble rim.

He took a bottle of aspirin from the medicine cabinet, shook two into her hand, and filled a glass from the tap. When she had taken the pills, he kissed her nose. "I'm sorry you have a headache. You slip into the tub, love, while I go pour us a glass of wine." His fingers skimmed the side of her face, and he brushed the softest of kisses across her lips.

Never had he felt so heartsick, Sam thought as he walked to the bar in the living room. Or so damned helpless. The look in Max's eyes was killing him. He'd give anything to be able to put back the spark, the impudent sass. She looked defeated. He could feel her pain. And he knew what caused it.

He hadn't meant to spy on her. Oh, hell, if he were honest, maybe he did intend to snoop a little. He'd told himself that he needed to go to the hardware store and pick up some extra screws for the pet door he and Manuel had made for Dowser this morning. It wasn't a coincidence he'd seen Max coming out of the bank. Concerned because she'd been gone longer than he expected, he'd circled through town three or four times until he'd spotted the blue Ram Charger. Keeping well out of sight, he had followed her and watched her enter another bank, the same one he used locally. Through the window, he had watched her speak with the loan officer, watched her as she left, dejected. She had been trying to borrow money.

An ache filled his chest. If she needed money, why hadn't she come to him? He would give her whatever she needed. Hell, he'd give her everything he had. Or loan it to her, with interest, if her damnable pride demanded it. But he couldn't stand to see her so dispirited over a problem so easily solved.

Now he was between the proverbial rock and hard place, a real avoid-avoid dilemma. If he offered her the money she needed, he'd have to explain how he knew about her business. She would be hopping mad if she knew he'd been playing Sam Spade. Yet, on the other hand, he couldn't tolerate ignoring her need.

Damn!

He'd come within a hair of having his banker call Max and say they'd changed their minds, that the bank would lend her whatever amount she wanted. But Sam knew she would be suspicious, and God help him if she ever found out he was behind it.

Still groping for a subtle way to broach the subject, he poured two glasses of the Zinfandel Max liked so much and walked back to the bathroom.

One limp arm flung over the side, Max lay in the scented water, eyes closed and bubbles clinging to her chin. Love for her swelled in him so hard and fast, it was almost painful.

"Angel," he whispered.

She didn't stir.

Disoriented, Max blinked and looked around. She was in bed. How had she gotten there?

Across the room in an easy chair, Sam sat reading the Stephen King novel she'd seen on his night stand. The lamp beside him reflected the red-gold highlights in his hair and cast a soft glow over his rugged features. One of the baskets of roses from the cottage rested on the table and their scent lent a sweetness to the air. He had remembered to bring them for her. She should have thought to ask him to pick up her guitar.

He must have sensed she was awake, for he looked up and there was an indescribable softening in his face. Max felt happiness well up and sweep over her. To have this wonderful man love her was far more than she deserved.

"Did you have a nice nap?"

She nodded. "My headache's gone. How long have I been asleep?"

"A couple of hours." He rose, walked to the bed, and stretched out beside her on his stomach. His finger traced the swell of her breasts, just visible above the fold of the sheet.

His touch pebbled her nipples and caused a little undulating contraction of her belly. "I don't remember getting out of the tub."

"That's because, my lovely water witch, you went out like a light. I had to haul you out of the bubbles before you dissolved like a sugar cube." His finger continued stroking back and forth, each pass pushing the sheet lower until it clung to the tips of her breasts, each pass rippling her belly and tightening her nipples. "I'm sorry you had such a lousy day. Are you sure that I can't do anything to help?" He dropped his head and began to trace the same path with his tongue.

"Not a thing," she said, her voice low and breathy.

"I'd be happy to help you line up a driller or arrange financing if you need it."

"Everything's under"—she gasped as his mouth encompassed a sensitive tip—"control."

He brushed his cheek back and forth over the wet crest. "Are you hungry? Loma left our dinner in the oven."

"Later," Max said. "Later."

He laughed and shifted his attention to her other breast. With languid tongue and unhurried hands, he loved her slow and easy. When they came together it was a soft dance, a lazy, wondrous feast that nourished the senses and the soul as well as the body.

Later they filled plates in the kitchen and ate dinner in Sam's big bed. Max had discovered a huge television behind a sliding panel in the bedroom and, after checking the program guide, had insisted that they watch *The Beast with Five Fingers*.

"I can't believe you're going to watch another old monster movie," he said.

"Sure I am." She snuggled under the crook of his arm. "I think I've about got this thing licked."

At ten o'clock the next morning, Max, dressed in slacks, loafers, and an oversized red cotton sweater, sat waiting for Jerry Bob Bossart, owner of Tip Top Motors. His Yellow Pages ad had promised top dollar for cars and trucks in good condition. "Try us first," his advertisement had urged.

Perched on the edge of a chair beside the cluttered desk, she chewed on her lip and wound the strap of her shoulder bag around her finger. Even though the window unit in the office trailer made a valiant effort, the air was heavy with the smell of yesterday's onions and stale cigar smoke. She doubted that the floor had been vacuumed since Jimmy Carter was inaugurated.

Maybe she'd made a mistake coming here, she thought, eyeing the purple Texas-shaped ashtray balanced precariously on a pile of papers a foot and a half high. It was overflowing with cigar and cigarette butts. She would have emptied it, except that the wastebasket was full of newspapers and hamburger wrappers. Plaques on the wall proclaiming Jerry Bob to be a member of the Chamber of Commerce and little league sponsor of the Tip Top Tigers made her feel only marginally comfortable with her choice of a used car dealer.

She was almost ready to bolt when the door opened and a man in a white Stetson stepped inside. He stood no taller than her chin and was almost as wide. His western brass belt buckle must have been stapled to his belly button, because the pants spanning his funnel-shaped girth defied the laws of gravity.

"I hear you're looking for me, young lady. I'm Jerry Bob Bossart." He stuck out his hand.

Max offered her hand and relaxed when she looked into a merry face with laughing hazel eyes. It was an open, honest face. "Yes, sir, I am."

"You'll have to excuse the mess in this place." He compacted the trash in the wastebasket with one stamp of his lizard boot and dumped the contents of the ashtray on top. A gray cloud of ash particles billowed up and he fanned them away from Max. "My missus usually takes care of the office, but she's up in Dallas helping our daughter tend to our first grandbaby. Born two weeks ago yesterday. Cute little bugger he is too."

It only took a short time for Max and Jerry Bob to strike a deal for the Charger. The price they agreed on would be more than enough to get Goose Gallagher's rig out of hock and give her a comfortable cushion for emergencies. She even convinced him to throw in transportation to replace the truck.

"I need something cheap, but rugged enough for my work."

"I believe I've got just the thing," he said as they toured the lot, looking over the inventory sitting under plastic pennants flapping in the breeze. "It's not too pretty, but it runs good. Ed Stanley, who owns the feed store down the street, used it for huntin'. Traded it in just last week for a Bronco."

Max frowned at the vintage jeep. Recently painted in garish variegated greens for a camouflage effect, it looked like a relic from World War II surplus. But the tires were good. She got in, cranked it up, and drove it around the block. Its tattered top and seat covers were patched with duct tape in so many places, it was like sitting inside an aluminum can. The engine ran like new, but every time she hit a dip or a pothole, her teeth jarred. The vehicle was obviously built for durability and not for comfort. A comedown from the ride of the Charger, but it would do.

She and Jerry Bob signed the necessary papers and walked across the street to his bank. Max took twenty-five hundred dollars in cash and opened an account to deposit the remaining funds. When they walked back to the car lot, she gave the truck a last wistful look before she pulled away in the jeep. The Charger's blue body sat looking forlorn, abandoned. There was a lump in her throat the size of Kerr County. It was like saying the last good-bye to an old friend she'd never see again. Giving Dowser to the pound wouldn't have been any more painful.

Her only consolation was that perhaps no one would buy it for a few days. If she could get the well drilled in a hurry, maybe she could buy it back from Jerry Bob. She clenched her teeth, lifted her chin, and reaffirmed the wisdom of her decision.

The first thing she did was buy a new pair of stockings, the sheerest and silkiest she could find. The second thing was to drive to Goose Gallagher's place by the river.

He was sitting on the porch rocking and drinking beer. Max could have sworn he hadn't moved since last Saturday.

"Hiddy there, little lady. I'd about give you up." His face beamed with a broad, toothless grin, and he set down the can he was holding and stood. "Yes, sir, I'd about give you up."

"It took me a bit longer than I'd planned to raise the cash," she said, climbing the steps and sitting in the lawn chair with the missing webs. "I had to sell my Ram Charger. It was tough to have to do that, Goose. I loved that truck."

He nodded sagely and patted his knees as he rocked. "Times are hard nowadays."

They sat together in silence for several minutes, staring out at the green water of the Guadalupe as it flowed on its course. Sunlight shimmered across the gentle jade ripples reminding her of the light that came into Sam's eyes when he looked at her. It warmed her to think of it. How she loved him. And how she loved this land, this river. Those long years ago, the hill country had been her sanctuary, and the green memory of it had comforted her many a dismal day and scary night.

Only the rhythmic creak of the rocking chair, the rustle of wind through the trees, and an occasional cluck of a scratching chicken marred the quiet.

Maybe it was because Goose reminded her a little of her grandfather, or maybe it was the hypnotic effect of the river, or maybe it was just because she needed to talk to somebody. For whatever reason, Max began to speak. She told the old man about the father who hated her, berated her, kept her terrified. She related her struggles, her triumphs, her disappointments. She told him the whole story of her desperate need to find water on the Bartons' hill. She even told him how much she loved Sam.

"You could have asked your feller to help you out."

"I know, Goose, but it's important that I do this on my own."

He nodded and rocked and stared out over the water. "To shed the haint of your pa."

"I'd never thought of it just that way. I figured it was because I was so hell-bent determined and stiff-necked proud."

"Pride's a powerful thing," the old man said. "Some say it's a sin, but it ain't all bad. Sometimes it's the only poke that keeps us gettin' up every mornin'."

"Do you think we've got a chance of finding water on that hill?" Max asked, allowing doubt to creep in for the first time.

"Hell, yes, little lady," Goose said, and slapped his thighs. "If you're half the witcher Dal Maxwell was, we're gonna hit that sweet water vein and thumb our nose at 'em all."

She laughed and slapped her thighs in return. "Damned right, partner." She got to her feet and said, "How about I buy you some lunch, and then we'll stop off and liberate your rig."

Goose stood and started for the door. "Just wait till I get my teeth and I'll be right with you."

The two of them ate smothered steak and mashed potatoes and collard greens at the local cafe Goose directed her to. The old man seemed to know everybody there and he introduced Max to them all. "Dal Maxwell's granddaughter," he told them. "She's one of them gee-ologists. We're workin' together on a job south of town," he added with a cocky jerk of his bald head.

After Goose finished his second helping of lemon meringue pie, they went to the sheriff's office and made arrangements for the release of his equipment.

The old truck and its mounted drilling rig looked as if it had seen better days, but Goose patted the fender and said, "Don't you worry none about ol' Sal here. She's got a lotta life left in her. Give me a couple of days to get her greased up and purrin', and then we'll go to work."

Max was disappointed that they couldn't start right away, but they agreed that Goose would hire a helper and they'd meet on the hill just after sunup on Friday morning. She gave him a hundred dollars for incidentals and wrote down Sam's phone number in case he needed to contact her before then. Waving good-bye to the old man, she headed toward the cottage to pick up her guitar.

While she was there, Max stripped the bed and washed the linens. After putting the load in the dryer, she tidied the little house and cleaned out the refrigerator. The sight of a huge roll of bologna with its red bow brought a smile to her lips. She left it on the bottom shelf. She never wanted to see another bologna sandwich. Some of the other things that were starting to spoil she threw away, some she stored in the freezer, and others she packed to take to Sam's. As soon as the bed was remade, she collected her guitar and locked the door.

A few minutes later, she drove up in front of Sam's house and tooted the horn. Sam came out of the garage to meet her. His welcoming smile changed to a frown as he gave the garish jeep the once-over.

"Why are you driving this godawful thing? Where's your truck?"

Max had forgotten that he would demand an explanation. Thinking quickly, she said, "The truck was making funny noises, so I left it with a mechanic in town." She crossed her fingers behind her back in a childish gesture to abrogate the lie. "This one's a loaner. Here," she said, thrusting a sack into his hands. "I picked up the perishables from the cottage. Maybe Loma can use them."

"I knew I should have gone with you this morning. Angel, if you were having problems with the truck, why didn't you call me? I could have picked you up. You don't have to drive this . . . *M*A*S*H* reject."

"Oh, I don't know. I think it's kind of cute." She patted a spot on the hood that was a particularly bilious shade. "It sort of reminded me of your eyes."

"Angel—"

"Forget about the jeep, Sam. I don't mind driving it for a few days. Anyway, let me tell you my good news." She broke into a broad grin. "Everything is all set to begin drilling."

He shifted the sack to one arm and hugged her with the other. "That's great, sweetheart. When do we begin?"

She glanced up at him and shook her head. "Not *we*, Sam." She tapped her finger on her chest. "*Me*. This is my project, remember?"

"*Your* project. Gotcha." He grinned and snapped a salute. "Can't I even watch?"

"Mmmm," she said, as if pondering a weighty question. "Maybe. If you're very good."

"Oh, I'm good," he said, wiggling his eyebrows. "Come inside and I'll show you how good." He started striding toward the door with Max in tow.

Laughing, she dug in her heels. "Wait a minute, Casanova. I've got to get my guitar."

"I didn't know you played," he said as she retrieved the instrument from the back seat. "I've always wanted to make love to a guitar player."

They left the groceries in the kitchen with Loma, and Sam took her hand and drew her outside. "I want to show you something."

His arm around her, they leaned against the white board fence that encircled the pasture. He pointed to a small herd of sheep. Dowser was running among them, driving them this way, then that. A black-and-white border collie stood under a tree, patiently watching the Doberman's antics. Apparently thinking the sheep had had enough, the collie barked and Dowser ran to her side and lay down.

"Bess?" Max asked.

"Bess. Like someone else around here I could name, she has him wrapped around her finger. Or paw, I suppose it would be with dogs."

Max wound her arms around Sam's waist and laid her head on his shoulder. "Who has wrapped who?"

He laughed. "I was speaking of myself, but I hope it's mutual. Lord, I was lonesome for you today. This place is empty when you're gone. Don't go off without me again."

"I finished all my business this afternoon. I don't have to go anywhere else until we start drilling Friday morning."

"You have a driller lined up?"

She nodded. "I hired the most experienced well driller in these parts." She didn't think it was necessary to mention that the reason he was so experienced was because he was over eighty years old. Sam would have just fretted about it. "He was a friend of my grandfather's."

"Max, are you sure you don't need some financial help with this?"

She stiffened in his arms. "I've told you a hundred times, I can handle it by myself, Sam."

"Sweetheart, don't get in an uproar. It's just that I know how expensive drilling around here can be. I'll be glad to make you a loan if you need it. Strictly business, you understand."

"Thanks," she said, "but I have a little extra in the bank for emergencies." She pulled away and whistled for Dowser. He came running to the fence when he saw her. She dropped to one knee and petted him as he licked her face through the fence. "I see you have a new ladylove."

Dowser gave a tongue-lolling grin and looked back at Bess. Then he bounded away toward the cluster of sheep.

Max and Sam went inside to wash up for dinner. After they had eaten, they decided to dress and go to the opening of a western art exhibit by several of the local artists.

Sam knew a number of people there and introduced Max to them as "my special lady."

At the end of the evening, Max sighed as she watched him write out a check for a magnificent sculpture of a copper stallion she'd admired. Something in the power and the tones of the figure had reminded her of Sam. She could hardly take her eyes off it, but she hadn't meant for him to buy it.

"Humor me," he had said.

The statue cost more than she'd got for her truck. It was getting hard to be independent. She'd rather have her Charger.

After Sam was asleep, Max feathered a kiss on his forehead and slipped from the bed. She took her guitar and went out on the patio. The moon was especially bright and stars studded the sky like winking fireflies. Night sounds, soft and mysterious, blended in with the rush of the river over its rocky bed.

Strumming a few chords, Max began to sing in a husky, bluesy voice that was perfect for a country ballad.

When the night takes hold
And shadows fill my soul,
I chase my haunted dreams

With green, Guadalupe-green . . . cries.

Rocky river shining clear,
Texas hills I hold so dear,
Lovely memories always mean
It's green, Guadalupe-green . . . sighs.

Now your arms enfold me.
Come close to me and hold me.
I've found my love it seems
In green, Guadalupe-green . . . eyes.

Green, green, Guadalupe-green
Willow water wise.
Green, green, Guadalupe-green
It's the color of your eyes.

Sam stood in the shadows and listened with tears in those green eyes. He'd never heard anything more beautiful, nor had he ever been given a more precious gift.

Eight

When the last notes of the refrain drifted away over the water, Max looked up to see Sam standing beside her. For a moment neither of them spoke. Instead, they savored the magic that brightened the moon and pirouetted around them, weaving a wondrous spell.

"I love you, Angel." His voice was a husky whisper.

"And I love you," she answered, holding out her hand to draw him down beside her on the wide padded chaise. She laid down her guitar and snuggled in his arms, her head on his chest, his cheek on her hair.

Simply holding each other, they listened to the rippling water and the whisper of the trees, soft chirrs in the night. An intense emotional awareness wrapped them in invisible bonds as they breathed enchanted air flavored with a faint sweetness like dew-touched jasmine.

"I—I can't seem to find the right words," he said. "I could almost feel your soul when you sang.

God, the power of the music. And the words. They're simple, but the way they came out of you grabbed my heart like a fist."

"I suppose that's the reason I've always liked country music. It deals with complex emotions in simple ways that people can relate to. Most of it is about love or about pain of one kind of another. Blues and country songs reckon with pain a lot. I think it's because most people are hurting somewhere down deep. They have wounds and shadows and haunting memories, and they're all looking for love."

"Tell me about your shadows, Angel."

Talking to Goose about her childhood had given her a better perspective, greater distance, and made the telling of it to Sam easier.

"I really don't remember much about my early childhood except that I was terrified all the time. I told you that my father frightened me with monsters to keep me quiet and out of his way. I told you that he didn't like me very much. That was an understatement. He despised me. My very presence seemed to be an abomination to him. Nothing I did pleased him. And I tried. Lord, how I tried.

"By the time I started kindergarten, I'd somehow learned to cook and clean and do laundry in my childishly inept way. In school I was a model student with A's in every subject. I desperately wanted his love. Or at least his approval, but nothing I ever did was enough. I don't remember his ever being physically cruel, but his words hurt more than any blows could have. He constantly told me how stupid I was, how ugly, how helpless to make anything decent of myself. I wasn't allowed to have friends over or go anywhere, not even to Sunday School. I couldn't have dates when I got older. I became very much of a loner."

"I could kill the son of a bitch for what he did to you." Sam's voice shook with fury and his whole body was trembling.

With gentle fingers, Max smoothed the frown from his forehead and caressed his clenched jaw. "I told you, he isn't worth the bother. I know that now. And it wasn't all bad. I had my grandfather. But if it hadn't been for my wonderful summers with Gramps, I don't think I could have survived. He was gentle and kind and full of fun. Until I could earn my own money when I was older, he bought the only decent clothes I had, and he taught me about love and laughter and courage. When we used to walk the hills together, he talked to me for hours about inner strength and determination and pride. Gramps made me believe that I could do anything and be anything I set my mind to. He gave me my guitar and taught me to play. It became my friend and my solace. I've never been able to express my feelings very well, except with music."

"Sweetheart, you have a real gift. With your talent, you should be a professional."

She laughed softly. "I tried it once about a year and a half ago when I discovered that the prospects for a geologist were very grim. I had always fantasized myself as another Reba McEntire or Crystal Gayle or Janie Fricke. Unfortunately the fantasy was very different from the reality. Singing by oneself is not the same as singing in front of an audience. I had terrible stage fright. Worse than terrible. I couldn't even manage a croak from my throat and my fingers had to be pried from my guitar. It was awful." She shuddered at the memory and cuddled closer to Sam. "I'll stick with writing songs, thank you."

"Do you mean you've written others?"

"Tons of them. I even have an agent in Nashville, but I haven't sold anything so far. There are more songwriters in this country than there are rocks on Honey Bear's hill. I've learned not to get my hopes up."

"If the rest of your songs are as good as the one I heard, I think somebody would be crazy not to buy them."

She smiled. "I think you're prejudiced, but thanks for your confidence, Sam. You'll never know how much it means to have *someone* believe in me." Her hand slipped back and forth along the arm of his robe, the feel of the soft velour bringing tactile comfort. "It's one of the most important things in the world."

"I believe in you, love."

"Don't ever stop, Sam." She hugged him fiercely. "Please, don't ever stop."

"Never," he promised. "And nobody will ever hurt you again."

They walked across the cobblestones of the plaza, then Max stopped and stared at the tiny, battered mission before her. Fluted columns and Spanish arches decorated the weathered stone facade of the historical structure, which seemed out of time and place in downtown San Antonio. "It looks just like the pictures I've always seen, but I never dreamed it was so small."

"I can't believe you've never seen the Alamo."

"I suppose it's like New Yorkers who've never seen the Statue of Liberty. I think the only time I was ever in San Antonio was for a geology conference, and we barely got out of the hotel."

Earlier that morning when their conversation had turned to Texas history, Sam had been appalled that she'd never visited the famous Texas site. Nothing would do until he'd planned a trip to the neighboring city. Although it was little more than an hour away from Kerrville, they decided to pack a bag and stay overnight to enjoy the sights. Sam had phoned for hotel reservations while she changed into slacks and a bright blue shirt and pondered over what to take with her from her meager wardrobe.

Max had offered to let him drive the jeep, but Sam had held open the door of his Jaguar and shot her a you've-got-to-be-kidding look that made her giggle. Even before they checked into their room, he'd parked in a garage near the mission so that she could see it right away.

Sam stuck his sunglasses in the pocket of his brown knit shirt and shepherded Max toward the cherished shrine. Inside, thick walls shut out sunlight and traffic noise. The chapel was cool and eerie. The air was permeated with the musty smell of history and traces of anguish from those long dead.

Apprehension slithered up her spine and bumps popped out on her arms. "I can almost hear the echoes of the past," she whispered. "Shouts and screams and cannon's roar. Flame and lead raining down like sleet. There are ghosts here. Can you feel them?"

He hugged her to him and rubbed her arms to warm her. "It's strange how this place can affect you. I couldn't have been more than about six or seven years old when I first came here. I remember that tears came into my eyes, then I got angry. I wanted nothing more than to be magically transported back in time so that I could fight beside Jim Bowie and Davy Crockett. I closed my eyes and wished with all my might." He looked down at Max and smiled. "I was devastated when I opened them and saw only my mother retying my little sister's hair ribbon. I sulked the rest of the day."

Max laughed and they spent a few more minutes inside before they walked out into the courtyard where the sun chased away the shadows. "Tell me about your family. I know Adrienne is your older sister."

"I have two sisters. Adrienne is three years older than I, and she's married to Jim McFarland, an ex-jock turned insurance executive. They live in Dallas and have a teenaged daughter, Linda, who loves loud music and plans to be a brain surgeon this week. Last week I think she'd decided to be a truck driver.

"Susan came along two years after me. She's a geographer and lives in Washington, D.C. She works for one of the government agencies doing some kind of hush-hush work with maps."

"Sounds impressive," Max said. "Is she married?"

He shook his head. "Divorced. No kids."

"Do your sisters have green eyes like you?"

One corner of his mouth lifted in a smug little grin as he nodded. "You really like my eyes, huh?"

"I really do. It was the first thing I noticed about you. Well, maybe not the first thing."

One eyebrow lifted. "What was the first thing?" His tone was playfully suggestive.

"How big your foot was."

She dodged his swat on the bottom and danced ahead of him, laughing over her shoulder. They stopped and bought snow cones from a vendor across the plaza, hers strawberry and his, grape. They traded bites and argued over which flavor tasted best. When hers started leaking, they tossed them into a trash barrel and Sam whipped out his handkerchief to wipe her sticky hands.

"How are you related to the Bartons?" she asked as they walked back to the car.

"Buck is my mother's older brother."

"Are both your parents still living?"

"My mom is. She lives in a condo in Austin when she's not gallivanting around the world with some of her cronies. She's in London now. She always wanted to travel, and Dad promised her that they would once he retired. But he died the year before he'd planned to retire. Heart attack. They never got to do the fun things together. He was too involved with his business."

Max was quiet as he started the Jag and drove the few blocks to the hotel. "So you decided to retire early?" she asked at last.

"Yep. I expanded Dad's small construction firm and devoted every bit of my time and energy to making all the money I'd ever need. I intend to spend the next thirty or forty years taking life easy and enjoying my wife and family."

"But you don't have a wife." A terrible thought sucked the life from her face and settled like a lead ball in her stomach. Her eyes grew large. Dear God, surely he wasn't married. "Do you?"

He pulled to a stop beside a liveried doorman outside the hotel. A lopsided grin crinkled the corners of his eyes as he brushed her cheek with the back of his knuckles. "Not yet. That's something I wanted to talk to you about."

Before his comment fully registered, her door was opened and they were set upon by a retinue of obsequious hotel employees. Max was flabbergasted at the treatment. With all the bowing and scraping and smiling, you would have thought they were visiting royalty.

She let out a low whistle when she entered the suite. It was sumptuous. With pale sea-green carpet, soft and thick as mink, the room was a rich, eclectic blend of contemporary, oriental, and French antique. A pair of intricately carved gilt arm chairs flanked a long, low couch of flame-colored silk which looked soft and poofy enough to get lost in. Behind the couch stood a six-panel screen, so magnificent it took her breath away. Done in gold and vibrant colors and intricate inlays of mother-of-pearl, it was a delicate water scene with wading birds and water lilies.

A bowl of Fuji mums sat on an oriental dining table of finely polished burled wood, and a similar floral arrangement was on a low chest in the bedroom. The king-size bed was covered with a stunning silk spread embroidered with flowers and birds that reminded her of the screen in the living room.

After Sam dismissed the bellman, he came up behind Max. She was staring at the opulent bathtub with gold swans as spigots. Big enough for a basketball team and shaped like a huge salmon-colored shell, it was more a spa than a tub. And deliciously decadent. He put his arms around her waist and pulled her back against him. "Like it here okay?"

"What's not to like? It's like something out of *Architectural Digest.* Are you sure they don't have us mixed up with Andrew and Fergie?"

"Not likely," he said, nibbling on her earlobe. "You're prettier than Andrew and I'm taller than Fergie."

She chuckled. "The service is certainly great here. Even the manager nearly tripped over his toes welcoming us. Does everybody get that kind of treatment?"

"I hope so," Sam said, turning his attention to the side of her neck. "But I suspect it might be because I own a piece of the place."

"Ahhh," she said, partly in response to his comment and partly in response to the lovely things his tongue was doing.

"Angel, about what I was saying when we were interrupted by the doorman—it is something I want to talk to you about."

She considered playing dumb or coy, but she was neither. And she knew exactly what he was referring to. But, as wonderful as things seemed between them, their relationship was still too new to think of commitments. Plus, she had to get her life straightened out before she could seriously consider anything else. She'd told Sam about her father, but he could never understand the power of her need to prove her own self-worth once and for all. She had to "shed the haint of her pa" as Goose had put it. And she had to do it alone.

"Let's put that topic on hold for now, Sam. We need some time."

Sam didn't want to put the topic on hold. He'd known almost from the first that Max was the woman for him, the one he'd always imagined sharing the rest of his life with. They suited each other. Not only was their lovemaking beyond his wildest dreams, but they had lots of other things in common. They both loved the hill country, and they'd talked about all the places they would love to visit. Max had admitted to a secret yen to travel to Greece and Scotland and the mountains of Peru, all the same spots he wanted to see. He had the time and the money for them to do anything they desired. Nothing would please him more than to be able to lay the world at her feet and watch her smile. His chest swelled at the thought of it. Anything that money could buy or love could provide would be hers.

And he knew she'd make a wonderful mother. He could almost visualize a black-eyed little girl with golden curls. A smaller angel. Maybe a couple of boys. They would have an ideal life together.

If it were up to him, they'd be married before sundown. He didn't need any more time to figure that out. She was his. He was hers. Simple as that. Call it fate or call it karma. They were created for each other. He knew it. But convincing Max seemed to be another matter. He'd wait a while. But not too long. Maybe another day or two.

"For now," he agreed. He gave her neck a last playful nip and took her hand. "Come out on the balcony. I want to show you something." Outside, they leaned over their fifth floor railing and looked down at the scene below. "*Paseo del Rio*, Riverwalk. It's San Antonio's answer to Venice, but instead of canals, we have a channel of the San Antonio River."

Both sides of the meandering river were paved and hosted a variety of trees and plants. Blossoms and the multicolored umbrellas of sidewalk cafés lent a festive air to the quaint area where shops and restaurants rose to frame the slow moving water. Small barges filled with sightseers floated along the twists and turns and passed under the footbridges spanning the narrow channel.

"It's beautiful," Max said, leaning farther out and peering up and down the Riverwalk as far as she could see.

"And even better at night. We'll take a moonlight stroll if you like."

"Do we have to wait that long? I swear I can smell enchiladas all the way up here."

He laughed and took her hand. "You like Mexican food?"

"Love it."

They quickly unpacked and went down to find the sidewalk cafe that Sam swore had the best enchiladas in town.

Sipping margaritas while they waited for their order, Max played peekaboo with a baby in a stroller at the next table. The little dark-haired girl gurgled with delight, laughing and drooling around the finger stuck in her mouth.

Sam smiled as he watched the two of them. "You like kids?"

Max nodded. "I used to baby-sit when I was in high school and college. I even used to keep John and Darlene Ramsey's two little girls so they could get away for a weekend now and then. I miss them."

"Ever think about having any of your own?"

"Someday," she said, and turned her attention to the steaming plate of food the waiter placed before her.

After lunch they wandered through the shops along the Riverwalk. They stopped to peruse the offerings of a sidewalk art show, held hands and laughed at the outrageous sayings on the T-shirts a vendor offered. Sam insisted on buying her a lovely pair of silver earrings, and she selected a second pair for Loma. When she admired a window display of beaded evening bags, he pulled her inside the shop to look more closely. All of them were exquisite, but one she fell in love with. On a long silver chain, it was shaped like a butterfly and heavily encrusted with royal blue and kelly green beads that shimmered like colored fire. Over her protests, Sam told the saleslady to wrap it up.

"I like to buy things for you," he said when she continued to argue.

They took a slow ride down the river on one of the small water taxis and enjoyed the lazy afternoon. When the sun began to sink behind the buildings of the city, Sam leaned down and whispered, "I think we need a bath." Max looked startled and he laughed. "All I've been able to think about for the past two hours is you and me in that giant clam shell upstairs."

She fought back giggles as he laced his fingers in hers and took off at a fast clip back toward the hotel. "Hold it, Sam," she said, almost having to run to keep up with him. "My legs aren't as long as yours. I'm out of breath."

He stopped and looked down at her with a wry grin. "I am acting a little like a randy teenager. Sorry, it's just that I can hardly wait to . . ." He bent to whisper in her ear, telling her exactly what he wanted to do to every part of her body.

A warm flush spread over her and stained her cheeks. Her knees went weak and her eyes closed as she sucked in a gulp of air. "All that?" she managed to murmur.

"And then some," he said, his grin broadening, his eyebrow lifting suggestively.

Max lay against the back of the tub, arms stretched out along the rim to support her, legs still locked around Sam's waist. She couldn't have moved if the building were on fire.

"I think I may die," she said, the words a languid sigh.

"Me too." He rested his head on her shoulder and nuzzled her chin with his nose. "But what a way to go. Do you think the maid will be shocked if she comes in and finds us like this?"

"I can hear the announcer now. 'Couple croaks in giant clam shell. Details tonight at ten.' "

They both started to laugh, and Sam reached behind him to grasp her ankles. Sliding back, he lifted one of her feet, then the other, planting kisses on the soles of each. "We'd better get out. Your toes are shriveling." He gave one a noisy nibble, then hoisted himself up, pulling her after him.

After they had dried off, they wrapped themselves in the terry robes provided by the hotel and stretched out on the bed to nap before dinner.

It seemed only moments later that Max awoke with Sam tickling her nose with kisses. "Wake up, sleepyhead," he said. "I'm starving."

She stretched and blinked. "What time is it?"

"After eight, and my stomach sounds like a demolition derby is going on down there."

"Poor baby." She patted his tummy. "You want to call for room service?"

He shook his head. "I've made reservations at the restaurant upstairs. The food is excellent and they have a small orchestra. I thought you might enjoy it. Besides, I want to show you off."

They dressed quickly, Sam in a gray suit, Max in her blue silk dress. She wound her blond hair into a loose coil atop her head and added the silver earrings he'd bought for her that afternoon. While he knotted a tie in the same shade of blue as her dress, she transferred her wallet and lipstick into the butterfly evening bag and slipped on sling-backed heels that matched her full skirted dress.

"I'm ready," she announced.

Sam's gaze slid over her like a caress, pausing where the delicate fabric crisscrossed over her breasts. "You look beautiful, Angel." He ruffled the silver dangles of one earring. "These should be diamonds. Soon we'll buy you diamonds."

"I don't need diamonds, Sam."

"Humor me," he said, and tucked her arm in his. "I want to give you beautiful things." He barely took his eyes off her as they left the suite and rode upstairs to the elegant restaurant.

The maitre d' met them with effusive greetings and whisked them to a quiet table by the window where wine was chilling in a silver bucket. The night seemed to be made of magic as they drank champagne by candleglow and gazed out over the lights of the city. Sam pointed out Hemisphere Plaza and the Tower of the Americas.

Max's every sense was heightened as soft music played in the background. Never had Sam looked more handsome nor had his eyes been lit with such fire. The crystal seemed to sparkle like diamonds; the wine slipped down her throat like liquid gold. The veal in its delicate white sauce seemed to be the most delicious thing Max had ever tasted.

And when Sam led her onto the small dance floor, she melted against him. They moved together in perfect unison, as if they had been practicing for years. He was remarkably graceful for his size, and his lead was strong and sure. The smell of him was more heady than the fine champagne. They didn't talk as they glided across the floor. There was no need. At that moment there was only the two of them in a world of slow music and soft lights.

When the set ended, Sam gave her a little squeeze and brushed his lips across her forehead. "Want to go for a walk along the river?"

She nodded and he signed the check while she went to the ladies' room and repaired her lipstick. Sam was waiting for her outside the door.

"Have I told you how beautiful you look tonight?"

"About a dozen times, but tell me again." She smiled. "I love to hear it."

Tucking her arm in his, he led her from the restaurant, stopping along the way to assure the maitre d' that everything was excellent.

Outside, they strolled along the river and laughed

at a group of teenagers who were clowning around with gaudy tourist sombreros and maracas and singing "La Bamba" at the tops of their lungs and slightly off-key. They stood on one of the bridges spanning the river and watched the play of lights on the slow moving water.

Suddenly, someone jostled Max and she slammed against the stone rail. Sam grabbed her. "Are you all right?"

"My purse!" She looked around and saw a dark figure running off the bridge. "Sam, he got my purse!" Panic almost overwhelmed her. "My beautiful purse. And my wallet's in it."

Sam took off after the thief, his long legs eating up the distance between the short, dark figure and himself. Not to be outdone, Max ran after them, but her high heels slowed her down. She took her shoes off as she ran, hopping on one foot, then the other until she held them in her hands.

"Stop, thief!" she yelled as they ran along the river, dodging startled people and weaving through sidewalk tables.

The man knocked over a waiter with a tray of drinks as he dashed through one outdoor restaurant, and glasses crashed onto the concrete. Sam hurdled the mess and roared for the thief to stop. Max ran around the broken glass and cursed as she felt runs pop and slither up her legs.

But Sam was gaining on the thief. He made a swipe with his long arm and grabbed a handful of shirt as they ran close to the edge of the river. Sam jerked the bag from the young man's grasp as they struggled. Then the shirt ripped and Sam fell with a splash into the murky water as the thief slipped away into the night.

Max pushed through the crowd that had gathered and screamed for Sam. He came up sputtering in the waist-deep water. His suit was soaked, his tie askew, and his auburn hair was dripping rivulets down his face.

"Sam, are you all right?"

He held up the sopping remnants of a dark shirt. "He got away." Then he grinned and raised the other hand to display a soggy jeweled butterfly. "But I got your purse."

She laughed and the onlookers applauded as Sam waded to the edge. A couple of men helped him to the riverbank and slapped him on the back. Trailing puddles and shoes squishing, he walked over to her and executed a deep bow. His eyes crinkled with humor, he dangled the bag by its silver chain.

"I rescued this for you, fair lady."

Tears shimmered in her eyes. Never had she loved Sam Garrett more than at that moment.

Nine

Early the next afternoon, Max was in the kitchen kneading dough under Loma's careful direction. The plump little housekeeper was wearing her new silver earrings and chattering away about her grandchildren when Sam came in with his suit in a damp bundle.

"What mischief are you two lovely ladies plotting against Manuel and me?" he asked, laying his bundle on the kitchen counter.

Loma ducked her head and giggled. "Oh, Señor Sam."

Max winked at him and grinned. "Loma is teaching me how to make her famous cinnamon rolls. If you're very nice, I may let you have some for breakfast in the morning."

"I'm always nice," he said, returning her grin. "You've got flour on your nose." He brushed it away. "I'm going into town to see if the cleaners can salvage my soggy armor. Want to come along?"

She shook her head. "I want to finish these. Do you mind?"

"Whatever makes you happy, Angel. I won't be gone long. Do you want to do anything special tonight? We could go two-stepping at Lonesome Joe's. I do a mean two-step." To prove his words, he grabbed Max and made a few spirited strides around the kitchen, singing in a nasal twang.

"You idiot," she said, laughing as she held her flour-covered hands away.

"Or had you rather do the polka?" He switched to a loud and lusty version of "The Beer Barrel Polka" and whirled her around a few times.

"You're crazy, do you know that?"

"Crazy about you." He dropped a quick kiss on her lips and Loma giggled.

"Could we save the two-stepping for another night? I need to get to bed early. We start drilling at sunup tomorrow."

Sam started to say something, then seemed to think better of it. "Fine with me. I'll be back before you know it. We can go for a swim when I get home." He lifted her chin and gave her another kiss.

When he had gone, Max went back to kneading the dough, humming "Guadalupe-Green."

"I've never seen Señor Sam so happy," Loma said. "I think he loves you very much. And I think you love him, too," she added with a knowing smile. "Soon I think there will be a wedding and little *niños* in the house."

"Maybe," Max said, giving the dough a final pat.

When the rolls were ready for the oven, Max washed up and took her guitar out to the patio to play and watch for Sam. Dowser had come running when he heard the sounds of her strumming. After she'd given him a hug and a few pats, he settled at her feet to doze in the warm sun.

She couldn't remember a time in her life when she had felt so marvelous. Even the big Doberman was more content here. It was becoming almost impossible to imagine days and nights without Sam. Love made the difference. All the ugly shadows from her early years seemed far away now, as if they'd happened to someone else instead of her. Inside she felt as clear and bubbly as a cool spring rising from the rocks of the earth. She had new strength, a new purpose. Right now she felt as if she could stand toe to toe with Dracula and not even flinch.

Tomorrow she and Goose would hit that vein of water, and she could close the books on her old life. She could pay off her debts and she and Sam could start fresh. Oh, she knew she had only to ask and Sam would give her any amount of money she wanted. He'd made that very plain. But strangely enough, she wanted to prove something to him as well as herself. She didn't want him to think of her as a whining, helpless female who had to have a man to bail her out of trouble. It had been embarrassing to have him see her fall apart over the "monster" at the cottage. She wanted Sam's respect.

At the sound of a car coming, Max looked up expecting to see Sam's maroon Jag rounding the bend. Instead she saw her blue Ram Charger spewing a plume of dust in its wake. Shading her eyes with her hand, she frowned in puzzlement, then felt a sickening dread spread over her as she recognized the driver. She clutched the neck of her guitar with white-knuckled fingers as she watched Sam get out of the cab and slam the door. Fury had twisted his face into an angry mask. It was obvious that he knew she had lied about leaving the truck with a mechanic. Lord, how she hated confrontations, and she knew they were about to have a lulu.

Laying aside the guitar, she stood and took a deep breath as Sam strode toward her. The tendons in his neck were standing out, and she could practically see steam coming out of his ears.

"How the hell do you explain that?" he roared, jerking his thumb over his shoulder toward the truck.

Guilt overwhelmed her. She could almost feel herself shrink to the size of a kindergartner under Sam's livid glare, and Dowser whined and scooted under the chaise. She desperately wished that a giant hand would swoop down from the sky and whisk her away. She'd screwed up again.

"I'm waiting." He ground the words out between clenched teeth. "And it had damned well better be good."

"I sold it."

"Hell, I know you sold it. I found it sitting on a used car lot. I bought it back from Jerry Bob Bossart." His eyes flashed with green rage. "I want to know why in God's name you sold something you loved as much as you loved that truck. And I want to know why the devil you told me a bald-faced lie about it."

"I needed the money, Sam. For my business."

"Your business?" He gave a derisive snort. "That's the most ridiculous thing I've ever heard.

Hell, you didn't have to sell your truck. For once you could have swallowed that stiff-necked pride of yours and come to me. If you're so all-fired determined to go through with this idiotic venture of yours, I've told you a dozen times that I'd give you all the money you need to drill a hundred dry holes on that godforsaken pile of rocks."

Max felt her own anger begin to rise. How dare he stand there like some puffed-up toad and yell at her, make her feel like scum? He was beginning to sound exactly like her father. Her spine stiffened, her eyes narrowed to thin slits, and her chin lifted.

"You never really believed in my dowsing, did you? You think I'm some kind of weirdo to be indulged."

Most of the anger left his face. "Angel . . ." He reached out to touch her cheek.

"Don't you 'Angel' me." She knocked his hand away. "You don't think Goose and I are going to hit that vein, do you?"

"*Goose?*"

"Goose Gallagher. He's the driller I hired. *He* thinks I've located a vein. And when we find water, I hope you choke on every nasty word you've said, Sam Garrett. You can take your green eyes and all your greenbacks and stuff 'em." She started to stalk off, but Sam caught her by the shoulders and turned her to face him.

"Goose Gallagher? Surely you didn't do anything so stupid as hire that old sot," he shouted in her face. "Dammit, Max, you haven't got the sense God gave a billy goat if you'd do anything that *stupid!*"

He let out another frustrated string of graphic gutter words, each punctuated with *stupid*. His fingers shook with anger as they dug into the flesh of her arms.

She felt herself tremble and pale as his words rang in her ears. Suddenly, her father's face was superimposed on Sam's, and she relived old horrors. His sour breath turned her stomach as he railed at her, venom dripping from the words as he yelled in her face. *Damn stupid snot-nosed brat. You haven't got the sense God gave a billy goat. Stupid . . . stupid . . . stupid.*

"Don't call me stupid," she said.

"Hell, it is *stupid* if you're going to pin your hopes on Goose Gallagher! Everybody in the county knows that old coot's nothing but a broken-down drunk who couldn't find his butt with both hands."

"Don't call me stupid," she spat at him. "I'm not stupid. And don't you yell at me and curse me. You sound exactly like my father. I'm not going to take that kind of garbage ever again. Not from you, not from anybody!"

"Angel, I . . ."

Struggling from his hold, Max stepped back and glared at him. Her chest rose and fell with rapid breaths. Unshed tears stung her eyes and her stomach felt like a mass of writhing snakes. "Maybe," she ground out, her voice quivering, "you're the one who's stupid. Maybe Goose Gallagher and I just need somebody to believe in us."

She whirled and ran into the house with Dowser close on her heels.

Sam felt as if he'd been drenched with icc water. Dear God, what had he done? Hell, he knew what he'd done. He'd allowed his damnable temper to get away from him and he'd lashed out at the woman he loved more than life. Lord the pain in her eyes. His heart had split open when he realized how badly he'd hurt her. He'd only wanted to protect her, to shield her from disappointment, but he was no better than that son of a bitch who'd made her childhood a living hell. He wanted to cut out his tongue and burn it.

For all her tough exterior, he knew Max was sensitive, and he'd ripped the scab off a freshly healing scar. What a fool he was. What an ignorant jackass. Damn! He kicked at a rock.

But it had nearly killed him when he found out that she'd sold her truck. Here he was, wanting to lay the world at her feet, and she wouldn't even come to him when she needed help. It stuck in his craw. But he knew why she'd lied to him about it. She'd done it to keep him off her back, but like the thick-headed clod he was, he'd kept hammering away at her.

He ran shaking fingers through his hair. If he didn't do something quick, he was going to lose her. What was he going to do?

Beg for forgiveness, that's what. Grovel. On his knees if necessary. He took off at a lope for the house.

Max was cramming things into her suitcase when he entered the bedroom. She ignored him.

"Sweetheart, please forgive me," he said. "I'm sorry I said all those things. I didn't mean them. I was angry. You have every right to bash my head in." He took her in his arms, but she was stiff and unyielding. "Angel, I love you. Curse me, yell at me, but please don't leave."

With a finger under her chin, he lifted her face. She stared at him with eyes as cold and black and empty as a graveyard at midnight.

"Please let me go," she said. Her voice would freeze Old Nick himself. "I have to get my toothbrush."

Sam dropped his arms, but he dogged her every step, trying every tack he could think of to get through to her. She looked at him as if he were a bug, picked up her suitcase, and marched from the house. Outside, she retrieved her guitar and stowed her things into the battered jeep. Dowser looked from Sam to his mistress and back again, then jumped into the back of the vehicle. He laid his head on his paws and watched them with sad eyes.

"Love, if you're bound and determined to leave, at least take your truck instead of this pile of junk."

"No, thank you. I had intended to buy it back out of my profits, but you bought it. It's yours." Her face was devoid of expression.

Sam sighed with self disgust. He hadn't thought it was possible to feel any lower. Now he did. "Do you still have a key to the cottage? I heard in town that they caught the burglar last night. You should be safe there."

She revved the engine. "I don't need it. I'll find other accommodations."

"Angel, please don't go."

She stared straight ahead as she pulled away. Sam watched until long after she had driven out of sight, then turned and trudged back inside to his bedroom. In the middle of his king-size bed lay a pair of silver earrings and the butterfly purse. He picked up the bag and sat down on the side of the bed. Propping his elbows on his thighs, he held the beaded butterfly in his hands. The flash of the blue and green crystals seemed to mock him as he traced the wings with his finger.

Never had he felt so alone. So empty.

Max dropped her suitcase at the foot of the bed beside her guitar and set the grocery bag on the scarred imitation maple table. The deluxe unit at the Trail's End Motel wasn't much, but it had a kitchenette of sorts and it was clean and cheap. She'd been to three places before she found one that allowed pets.

After she'd wedged the TV dinner into the minuscule freezing compartment of the old refrigerator, and stored the few other essentials she'd purchased, she ran water into a battered pan she found in the cabinet and set it down for Dowser. She washed the plastic bowl she'd bought, filled it with dog food, and placed it on the worn linoleum.

Trudging over to the double bed, covered with a limp chenille spread in a faded dusty rose, she sank down on the swaybacked mattress and sucked in a deep, shuddering breath. She clenched her teeth so tight that her jaws ached, but she refused to give in to the lump that had been lodged in her throat since her fight with Sam.

Before she could start thinking about the things he'd said again, she snatched up the telephone and placed a call to her roommate.

"Beth, it's Max. Any activity there?"

"Oh, hi, Max. I was just going to call you." She

stopped to sneeze. "I stayed home with a cold today and the real estate agent brought a couple by this morning and another one this afternoon. I eavesdropped a little while they were here and both sounded interested. Maybe one of them will make an offer on the house."

"Maybe, but I've learned not to hold false hopes."

"Max, are you okay? You sound funny."

"I'm fine," she lied. "But you sound terrible. Have you called the doctor?"

"It's just a cold. All I need is aspirin, orange juice, and tissues."

The friends chatted a few more minutes and Max gave Beth the number of the motel in case there was any news. "I'm registered here as Angela Maxwell."

"Why the cloak and dagger bit?"

"It's a long story. I'll tell you another time. Take care of your cold."

After she hung up, Max lay back on the bed and stared at the brown water stains on the ceiling until it got too dark to make out the shapes.

Pain was beginning to replace the numbness in her heart. Despite her efforts to keep her thoughts on other things, Sam's anger and his hurtful words crept into her consciousness. They mingled with memories of her father's vitriolic accusations and chased around in her head until she couldn't tell one from the other. Ugly echoes attacked her from all directions, cutting, stabbing, bludgeoning until she uttered one long, soul-wrenching moan. Tears held at bay for hours burst their restraints and poured forth in deep sobs. She buried her face in a lumpy pillow and wept until she was exhausted.

Sometime later, Max came awake. The room was totally dark and the phone was ringing. She groped for the bedside lamp, then fumbled for the phone.

"Hello," she mumbled into the receiver.

"Angel, I've had a hell of a time trying to find you."

She didn't respond.

"Sweetheart, please talk to me. We've got to talk."

"I don't want to talk to you. It's over. I won't tolerate abuse from anyone ever again. Please leave me alone." She quietly replaced the phone in its cradle.

In less than a minute the phone rang again. She unplugged the cord and pushed herself off the bed. Shedding her rumpled clothes, she headed for the bathroom and a long shower.

After she'd dried off and put on her nightshirt, she padded barefoot into the tiny kitchen and opened the freezer. She looked at the TV dinner and frowned. It was too much trouble, she decided and reached for the bread and a jar of peanut butter. She was unscrewing the lid when there was a knock on the door.

She tiptoed over to it and made sure the safety chain was in place. "Who is it?"

"It's me. Sam. Let me in, Angel."

"I have nothing to say to you, Mr. Garrett. Go away and leave me alone."

Max walked back to the kitchenette and finished unscrewing the jar. The knocking continued, more insistent now. Ignoring it, she slathered crunchy peanut butter on a slice of whole wheat bread. The knock became a banging and the force rattled the thin walls. She grabbed a banana and stripped the peel away.

"Max," Sam shouted, "let me in. We've got to talk."

"I told you we have nothing to say," she yelled back, furiously slicing the banana into a layer of little circles on the peanut butter. Dowser whined and looked up at her from under the table. His eyes seemed pitiful, pleading. "I'm not letting him in," she said to the dog, and slapped another slice of bread on top of the bananas. "He's nothing but grief, and I don't need it."

"If you don't let me in, I'm going to break this damned door down!"

She threw down the knife and stomped to the door. "Sam, I said go away. It's almost eleven o'clock and people are trying to sleep. You're going to wake up the whole town."

"Then let me in, Angel. I'm not leaving until you do."

"No."

The banging started again.

"If you don't leave immediately, I'm going to call the police."

Sam started rattling the window beside the door. He thought she was bluffing. Well, she'd show the overgrown baboon she meant business. She strode over to the bedside table and jerked up the Kerrville directory. She quickly found the emergency number and dialed it. Nothing happened. The line was dead. Damn, she thought. She'd unplugged the phone. Sticking the cord back in place, she tried again.

When a man answered, she explained that someone she didn't wish to talk to was making a disturbance at the Trail's End Motel, unit number seven.

"A car will be right there," he said.

Max walked back to her sandwich and neatly sliced it in half. "Now he's in for it," she told Dowser. Ignoring the racket as best she could, she turned on the TV, poured a glass of milk, and took it and the concoction she'd made to bed. Sitting cross-legged on the dipping mattress, she focused her attention on a wavy black-and-white image of Johnny Carson and took a big bite of her peanut butter and banana sandwich.

When she saw the flash of red and blue lights over the top of the sagging draperies, she stole from the bed and peeked out the window. Sam was spread-eagled against the side of a police car. A twinge of remorse threatened to grow into something bigger, but she tamped it down.

"Serves the big ox right," she declared to Dowser, who stared at her with accusing eyes.

A dismal gray sky, sprinkled with dying morning stars, hung over the hills as Max urged the jeep up the steep incline to the drilling site. Dawn was almost an hour away but, since sleep had eluded her, she decided she might as well wait for Goose as toss and turn on the creaking, sagging instrument of torture at the motel.

Pulling to a stop beside a tall, twisted juniper, she snagged the paper sack beside her and got out. Dowser raised up, looked around, then curled back into his comfortable spot in the rear and closed his eyes.

Envious of the Doberman's ability to sleep, Max withdrew the large styrofoam container from the sack and sipped the coffee she'd bought at a truck stop. The hot, bitter brew revived her only marginally. Her eyes felt gritty, her body buzzed with fatigue, and her stomach seemed to be full of ball bearings. Through the restless night, her mind had been in too much turmoil to rest. Shadows had filled her soul, but green memories couldn't chase them away. Now green memories were the shadows that haunted her. Every time she closed her eyes, Sam's face swirled into view. Sam's face. Sam's green eyes. Angry. Accusing. Mocking.

Oh, she could have dealt with the anger well enough. Since she'd met Sam, she seemed to have developed a temper herself. And even though she didn't like confrontations, she could hold her own. Hadn't she been the star pupil in the assertiveness training class in college? But she couldn't tolerate his attack on her self-esteem. It had taken three long years at the University Counseling Center to begin to repair the damage from her father's abuse, to discover her own self-worth, to learn to believe in herself. But the events of the past two years had begun to erode her confidence, and she refused to allow Sam to undermine it even further. She was *not* some kind of weirdo, nor was she a silly, simpering female without sense enough to take control of her own life.

She wandered over to the boulder and leaned against it, drinking the strong coffee and looking out over the hills at the lightening sky. As the stars faded, a few wisps of pink began to stain the horizon, and a light breeze carried the sharp scent of evergreen and dew-fresh laurel. Only an occasional rustle in the underbrush marred the absolute stillness on the hard, rock-strewn hill. This place had stood waiting for many a sunrise, had witnessed countless comings and goings. It endured. Changing and adapting, but strong and proud. She had weathered rough spots before; she would again. She would endure as well. She was a survivor.

Even if Sam thought she was a superstitious flake engaged in a fruitless and idiotic venture, she was *not* stupid. She *knew* there was water beneath her feet. She believed in Max Strahan, even if he didn't. Goose Gallagher had more faith in her than Sam did. Well, she and Goose were going to hit that vein, and when they did she was going to thumb her nose at Sam Garrett and get on with her life. It would take more than a soured love affair to stop her.

As Max watched the breaking dawn she focused her thoughts on positive things, dwelling on the future instead of the past, planning how she would spend the money she received from Buck Barton. Why, she might even go to Nashville. Songs about love gone wrong were always popular. She could certainly put her heart into a couple of those.

Max glanced down at her watch and chewed the side of her lip. It was eight-thirty. Sunup had come and gone. Where was Goose? They should have started drilling long ago. Had his rig broken down? Had he been in an accident? Her worried mind started to conjure up all kinds of dire images.

Just when she'd decided to go looking for him, the sound of an engine on the road below reached her ears. It was Goose. She breathed a sigh and gave a nervous laugh of relief. Smiling broadly, she stood waiting for the rig's assent.

But it was not Goose and ol' Sal that pulled to a stop and blocked the road. It was a blue Ram Charger with Sam Garrett at the wheel.

Max's smile faded, but she stood her ground as he walked toward her. He was wearing jeans and the same green-and-blue-striped shirt he'd worn yesterday. But it was rumpled and the tails hung out. His hair was disheveled, as if he'd run his fingers through the auburn waves a thousand times. Pain stabbed her when she saw how bloodshot his eyes were, and she almost cried out to him, almost pulled him into her arms to comfort him. But she balled her fingers into tight fists and clenched her teeth together.

When he stopped before her, she asked, "What are you doing here? Did you come to watch the drilling?"

"No," he said, his voice low and husky. "I came to talk to you, and I'm not leaving until I do. You can't call the cops up here."

She dropped her gaze as a rush or remorse coursed through her. "Did they take you to jail?"

"No, I explained the situation and they let me go." He was quiet for a moment. "Angel, look at me." She raised her eyes. "I can't let you throw away something so precious because of one quarrel. I never meant to hurt you. I lost my temper and said some dumb things. I can't take the words back. And I can't promise that we won't ever argue again. Most couples with strong personalities argue at one time or another. It's unavoidable when two people are as hardheaded and opinionated as we are. But, sweetheart, I'm not like your father.

There's one big difference." He reached out and stroked her cheek with the back of his fingers. "I love you with all my heart."

Her throat constricted and tears glazed her eyes. It would be so easy to fall into his arms and convince herself that their problems had magically disappeared. But it wasn't that simple. "Sam," she asked, her voice barely a whisper, "do you believe in me?"

"Of course I believe in you. I believe in you in a hundred ways. I know that you're a wonderful, passionate human being with tremendous talent and a gift for love and laughter and caring. You're strong and proud and determined."

"But do you believe in me when I tell you that I *know* there is water on this hill? Clear, good water less than a hundred feet beneath where we stand?"

His hand cupped the side of her neck and his thumb brushed along the ridge of her jaw. He looked up and away from her, and she watched his Adam's apple as he swallowed. Then his eyes met hers again. She could see the misery there. "To be honest, I don't know. For your sake, Angel, I want to believe it. I don't want you to be disappointed. My heart tells me yes. But my head tells me . . . no."

She closed her eyes as anguish ripped through her. He couldn't suspend his disbelief. Not even for her. "I see."

"Are you going to let this one thing keep us apart? I refuse to let you do that. Max, we love each other. We can have a wonderful life together. You don't have to rip your heart out over this damned hill. I'll give you any amount of money you want. You won't have to worry about debts or eat bologna sandwiches ever again."

"That's the problem, Sam. *You'll* give me. I must do this on my own. I need to know that I can, and I need to know that you think I can. It's a matter of respect for my integrity." She stepped back. "You'll have to go now. I'm expecting Goose at any minute."

"He's not coming."

Her eyes widened. "What do you mean, he's not coming?"

"Goose Gallagher is in jail."

Ten

All the blood drained from her face. Black spots danced in front of her eyes. For a moment Max thought she might faint, and she'd never fainted in her life.

"In jail? Is this some sort of sick joke?"

Sam shook his head. "You must have given him my number, because he called for you this morning. He asked me to tell you there'd been 'a little hitch in his plans.' They got him for public intoxication."

Fury rolled over her. "Why didn't you tell me right away?"

"Because I wanted a chance to talk to you first."

"Damn you, Sam Garrett. Damn your rotten hide. You ought to know how important this is to me, and here you've been reciting pretty speeches while all the time you knew. And if you say 'I told you so,' I'll throttle you. Get out of my way!"

"Where in the hell are you going?" he called after her as she stalked toward the jeep.

"To the jail," she yelled. "And if you don't move *your* truck, I swear I'll run right over it."

"I'll go with you. Maybe I can help."

She whirled and glared at him. "You stay out of my business. I can handle it myself."

Sam pulled the Charger into the clear just as Max came roaring by. She hadn't missed him by more than inches. He got out and watched her tawdry jeep bounce down the rough road, spitting gravel and kicking up a trail of dust. "Damned fool woman! You're going to kill yourself," he shouted after her.

Dowser came running from the other side of the hill. He looked around, then sat at Sam's feet and whined.

"Looks like you're stuck with me, boy. Get in." He held open the door while the Doberman jumped inside. "At least she's talking to me even if she is yelling. Think that's a good sign?"

As Max pulled into a parking place near the jail and got out, a horn honked behind her. Incensed when she turned and saw Sam, she put her hands on her hips and glared at him. "I thought I told you I would handle this."

He shrugged and grinned. "I just wanted to tell you that you forgot your dog." Dowser stuck his head out the window and gave a little woof of greeting. "I'm taking him home with me until you come up with the ransom." With that parting salvo, he drove off.

Max kicked the side of the jeep and uttered a rude oath. Oh well, she'd deal with that later, she thought as she headed for the jail.

Since it was his fifth offense, Max paid nearly two hundred dollars in fines to spring Goose. So far he had cost her almost half the proceeds from the Charger, and they had yet to put a bit to the ground. Sober and contrite, he was quiet as she drove him back to Goodtime Moe's to pick up his truck.

When she pulled up beside the battered vehicle in the seedy tavern's empty parking lot, she asked, "Goose, what happened? I was depending on you."

The old man hung his head. "Well, little lady, I run into a problem. I tried to find me a helper, but most of the ones I knowed real good was dead or too stove up to work anymore. The other ones I offered to hire laughed right in my face. Thought I was pulling their leg, called me a crazy ol' coot. I couldn't find nobody. It was then that the miseries come upon me, and I tried to whup 'em back with Wild Turkey. Never could handle bourbon. Not even the good stuff. I musta got a little rowdy, 'cause I woke up this morning in the tank. I feel right bad I let you down, you countin' on me and all."

Fingers beating an impatient tattoo on the steering wheel, Max thought a moment. "Goose, if I can find someone to help you, could you be ready to start this afternoon?"

"Yes sir-ee bob." The animation came back to his wrinkled face as he slapped his thigh. "Ol' Sal's purrin' like a kitten and rarin' to go. I'd be much obliged if you could dig up somebody to lend a hand."

After practically making him swear in blood to appear at the site, sober and ready to drill, as soon as she could locate an assistant, Max dropped Goose off and stopped by the drilling company where Mary Lou worked. As soon as she heard

Max's problem, the affable yellow-haired woman called a student at the local college who occasionally worked for their company. He had just come in from his morning classes and agreed to help. The young man promised to go by Goose's house after lunch and help him move the old cable tool rig to the hill.

"That boy's real dependable," Mary Lou said. "And strong as an ox. Jim Clay will give you a good day's work."

On her way back to the motel, Max dropped by a florist and made arrangements for a small bouquet and a thank you note to be sent to Mary Lou. She considered going to pick up Dowser, but decided to leave him at Sam's. She hated for the big Doberman to be cooped up in the tiny motel room. He'd be happier romping with Bess and chasing sheep for a day or so, and she knew he'd be well cared for.

In any case, she was not in any mood to deal with any more of Sam's brand of persuasion. She was too vulnerable to his tactics. On the hill this morning, she'd been a hair's breadth away from melting into his arms until he'd told her about Goose. The way things were going so far, she was beginning to doubt herself. Maybe she was chasing rainbows. Maybe she ought to give up the whole crazy idea. No. She refused to let a few roadblocks get her down. She was strong, she reminded herself. She could do anything. There was water on Honey Bear's hill, and she was going to prove it to Sam Garrett if it was the last thing she did.

* * *

By two o'clock, Max was sitting on the boulder tossing blue juniper berries at a prickly pear cactus that clung to a pocked ledge in the rock. Her whole body was zinging with anticipation. *This is the day, this is the day,* her supercharged brain intoned. *We're going to do it.*

It was not long before she heard the old truck lumbering up the hill. Goose was at the wheel herding the vintage vehicle over the rise and into the clearing. Devoid of windshield and fenders flapping, it had tires so thin she could almost see the air. Behind him, caution lights flashing, was a shiny black pickup with a half dozen extra fog and running lamps, a roll bar, and a grille grinning with chrome. Its driver, Max discovered when the old man and the younger one got out and came toward her, was Jim Clay.

"Yes sir-ee bob, me and Jim boy here are gonna make a good team," Goose said, patting the muscled shoulder of the shy blond giant beside him. "Where you want us to rig up?"

Max pointed out her row of markers and they selected the best spot. "How long do you think it will take, Goose?"

"How deep did you say?"

"Seventy-five to a hundred feet. Probably closer to seventy-five."

Max noticed that Jim cut his eyes to her in a questioning manner, but when she ignored him, he shrugged as if to say, "As long as I get paid, you're the boss."

Goose stroked his grizzled whiskers. "Well, we'll set 'er up and get started today. And near as I can figure, we ought to be done before sundown tomorrow."

Max took a soft drink from the cooler and stepped out of the way so the men could go to work. The pair moved the rig in, leveled it, and raised the derrick, using a cathead and ropes to hoist the tall structure. She was astonished to see that Goose could swing a sledgehammer nearly as well as Jim as they pounded stakes for the guylines into the hard rock. Terrified that the old man was going to keel over with a heart attack from the exertion, she almost intervened, but Jim beat her to it. In his quiet way, the young man eased Goose into another task while he set the stakes.

After what seemed to take forever, with Goose cursing and cajoling and greasing and oiling, the old propane-powered motor coughed to life and everything was made ready to begin the drilling.

The roar of the engine and the pounding, pounding of the spudder echoed over the hills and through the arroyos as the assault on the limestone began. Max watched the young man and the old one lift a huge wooden spool from the bed of Jim's truck. They set it up near the rig and poked a tattered beach umbrella through its middle to make a table.

Mopping sweat from his bald head with a frayed handkerchief, Goose walked over to Max. "We got 'er goin'," he shouted over the racket. "Ain't much you can do around here, little lady. Me and Jim's gonna play a little gin while Sal does her work." He glanced up at the late afternoon sun. "We'll shut her down about dark and start up about daylight."

Max hesitated to leave her project, but Goose was right. It was out of her hands now. Promising to see him the next day, she left. As a treat, she detoured by the video store and rented a tape player and two of the most gruesome horror movies she could find. They would keep her mind off the drilling. Maybe they would even keep her mind off Sam.

A hundred times today, she'd caught herself wishing he was on the hill to share the excitement with her. She could close her eyes and imagine the warmth and pressure of his arms around her as she leaned back against his chest, almost hear his husky laughter rumble in her ears. Oh, Sam, she thought with a sigh, why couldn't you understand? Was she expecting too much of him? Was her pride so important?

Sitting in bed at the Trail's End, she ate a lonely supper and watched one of the films she'd rented. Not once did her hair rise or heart palpitate. In fact, it was kind of boring.

Before she could begin the next one, the phone rang. When she answered, Sam said, "Dowser and I miss you."

The sound of his voice, lazy and seductive, tripped a flood of feelings deep inside. She almost blurted out, "I miss you, too," but stopped herself. "I thought he might enjoy some time with Bess and the sheep if you don't mind. I'll pick him up on my way out of town Sunday."

"You're leaving?"

She swallowed and tried her darnedest to keep the quiver out of her voice. "Yes. Goose started drilling this afternoon, and he thinks we'll be finished by late tomorrow if everything goes well. I have business in Houston that I need to take care of on Monday." She didn't add that with any luck she could pick up the check from Buck Barton and save her house from foreclosure.

"Why don't you come over for dinner tonight? Loma's frying catfish hoping you'll come."

"I've already eaten," she said, glancing at the remnants of a TV dinner on the bedside table. "But thank you anyway. And thank Loma for me."

"Angel, I love you," he said with an intensity that wrenched her heart like a fist. "I love you more than life. There will never be anyone for me but you. Please come back to me. Give us another chance." When she didn't respond, he said, "I'll be here. Waiting for you."

Max held the phone to her ear for a long time after he hung up, listening to the taunting buzz, unmindful of the tears running down her cheeks. Someday soon he would find someone else. Someone more worthy of his love than she. Someone with a nice, normal background and a good family. Someone who wasn't as different as she was or as tied up with monsters and witching sticks.

This pain would all pass. It was for the best.

It seemed as if Max had gone up and down the hill a dozen times during the day checking on their progress. She'd been there, nervously drinking coffee from a paper cup, when Goose and Jim had started drilling again at daybreak. She'd watched Goose check and adjust the cable with gloved hands fine tuned, after years of experience, to the subtle differences in tension. She'd watched him flush and bail the cuttings from the hole, and she'd listened to the constant pounding of the tool until the noise reverberating in her head made her feel like a punch drunk fighter.

"It'll be a while yet, little lady," Goose shouted

each time over the clamor, unendingly patient with her anxiety as he reported fifty feet, sixty feet, seventy feet.

The old man had told her they'd been lucky not to hit much flint and the drilling was going especially well, but Max thought the process was taking forever. By the time he hit seventy-five feet and stopped to bail the hole, she was a bundle of nerves. Unable to do more than stare at the pictures, she threw down the magazine she'd bought at the drugstore on one of her myriad trips to town and began to pace. She was unaware of the tall, auburn-haired figure on the next hill, partially concealed by a scrub oak and holding binoculars to his eyes. He was every bit as nervous as she was.

When the pounding began again, Max closed her eyes and prayed to every saint she could think of. And she wasn't even Catholic. She forced herself to sit down in one of the ragged lawn chairs by the makeshift table and read an article about newly discovered Mayan ruins, but the words might as well have been in Bulgarian for all the sense they made to her.

The shadows were getting long when Jim yelled, "Look at that!"

Max jumped up from her chair as if she'd been shot."What? What?"

Jim pointed. The string of tools was completely slack.

"What does that mean?"

"Might mean we've hit a cave," Goose said solemnly. "Or," he added with a wry grin, "it might mean we've hit the vein."

Max held her breath as he ran the bailer down. "Well?" she asked a few minutes later.

"Seventy-eight and a half feet. Water, cool and sweet as any I've seen. It'll pump thirty, thirty-five gallons a minute." He was grinning from ear to ear.

Max let out a whoop that could be heard in San Antonio. Laughing and dancing around, she hugged Jim, then she hugged Goose and planted a smacking kiss on each of his wrinkled cheeks. "We did it, Goose! By damn we did it!"

The old man looked enormously pleased with himself as Jim chuckled and shook his head in disbelief. Goose shut off the motor and said, "Put your ear to the hole. Mind the grease now," he cautioned as she ducked between the crossbars of the derrick.

Max didn't care about the grease. She held her braid with one hand and put her ear to the well. Her eyes grew wide and a look of awe came over her face. "I can hear it, Goose. I can hear the water rushing."

"You're Dal Maxwell's grandkid, all right," the old driller said. "You hit it right on the money. A few yards either way and we coulda missed it." At the sound of tires crunching on gravel, he glanced up and said, "It looks like we got company."

When Max saw Buck Barton and a tall, gray-haired woman getting out of a Suburban, she scrambled clear of the derrick and ran toward them, wiping her greasy hands on the seat of her jeans. The gruff old wildcatter introduced her to Olive Barton, Honey Bear.

Max grinned. "I'm glad to finally meet Honey Bear. I've heard a lot about you."

The woman returned her smile, her blue eyes twinkling with humor. "And I've heard a lot about you. I understand you're the one who's going to drill a well on my hill."

"No, ma'am," Max said seriously. When Honey Bear's smile began to fade, Max broke into an even broader grin. "It's already drilled. We just hit water. All you'll ever need."

Buck let out a loud guffaw and hugged his wife under one beefy arm. "Hot damn! I told you I had a feeling about this little gal. Let me get my checkbook."

It was already dark when Max put the key in the lock of unit seven and opened the door. Grimy, greasy, and worn to an emotional nub, she dumped her belongings on the table and started for the shower. She was just unlacing her boots when the phone rang.

Her first thought was: Sam! She snatched up the receiver before the second ring.

She was disappointed when a man with a nasal twang said, "Max, this is Smith Bullock in Nashville. Glad I finally caught up with you. I've been trying to reach you all afternoon."

When she recognized that it was her agent, she said, "Sorry about that, Mr. Bullock. I've been out drilling a water well."

"To each his own, I suppose," he said, and cleared his throat. "Say, lady, I've got some good news for you. Are you sitting down?"

Max felt her heart skip a beat. "Yes," she replied, waiting.

"I've just sold five of your songs to one of this town's leading female recording stars for her new album. She went ape over your stuff. And she wants to look at anything else you've got."

When he told her the name of the singer, Max's mouth dropped open. She was one of Max's favorites, and almost every album she cut went to platinum. Her mouth dropped even farther when she discovered the "sweet deal" her agent had made for her.

"Cat got your tongue?" he asked when Max was too stunned to reply. "Max?"

"I'm here. I'm just in shock. I can't believe it."

Smith Bullock laughed. "Believe it, babe. When word gets out about this, you're going to be in big demand. You're on your way. When can you have something else to me?"

"Let me have a couple of days for this to sink in, and I'll get back to you."

She sat on the side of the sagging mattress and stared at the toes of her dusty boots. She couldn't believe it. She, Angela Maxwell Strahan, was an honest-to-goodness, bona fide, professional songwriter. Arms outspread, she fell back on the bed with a silly grin pasted on her face. For so long it had only been a dream. Now it was reality.

Say, that was a great line for a song. Only a dream. Or had that been used? She finished pulling off her boots and did a little strutting jig to the bathroom.

The phone was ringing again when she shut the water off. She quickly wrapped her wet hair in a turban and grabbed a second towel as she dashed for the night table.

"Hello," she answered, holding the phone against her shoulder as she dried off.

"Max, it's Beth." Her roommate sniffled and asked, "Did your agent reach you? I gave him the number there."

"Yes, and you'll never guess what he wanted." Max related the story to Beth's excited squeals and interjections of, "You're kidding! That's fantastic!"

"And on top of everything else," Max said, "we hit water today." She told Beth about their find. "It must be my lucky day. I don't see how anything could get any better." *Yes, you do*, a little voice in her head said as a picture of laughing green eyes flashed in her mind.

"Well, hold on to your hat, roomie," Beth said. "I've got some more news for you. The real estate agent just called and he has a contract on the house for your asking price."

"For real?"

"For real. There's no question of the client's credit, and the family wants to move in by the first of next month."

"I can't believe this. It can't be happening. Now that I don't have to sell the house, it's sold."

"You want to back out? He said to let him know by tomorrow."

"Yes. No. I'm not sure. I don't know what I'm going to do. Heck, I may even move to Nashville now. I'll have to think about it. My brain's on overload."

After she hung up, Max walked around in a daze. She put on a robe and dried her hair. "It's a dream," she kept saying. "It's only a dream."

Hairbrush in hand, she sat on the side of the mattress. The creak of the bedsprings and the hum of the refrigerator were the only sounds she heard as she stared at the walls of the small, shabby room. Everything she'd been praying for had come to pass. She should be happy. She'd made a huge profit with the well, and Honey Bear had been so delighted, Buck had thrown in a five thousand dollar bonus. The house was going to sell; her secret dream of being a songwriter had come true. She was a success in anybody's book. And she'd made it on her own.

But now that the initial hoopla had died down, she felt strangely depressed. A deep, dull melancholy abraded her spirit. Why wasn't she happy?

Sam.

Her accomplishments were empty without Sam to reflect her joy and share in her triumph. She'd done everything she'd set out to do; her pride had been restored. But pride was a cold lover. And hollow-hearted loneliness was a high price to pay for it.

Pride. Gramps had always said she had more than her share. Sam, too, had cursed her stiff-necked pride. Yet most of her life it had helped her survive the hostile harangues of her father, and without it she would have buckled under the pressure of the past two years. Yes, she'd saved her pride, wrapped it around her like a protective mantle. But there was no warmth in it.

She thought of Sam's hurtful words and she thought of her father. As she pulled the memories back and examined them, a new understanding began to dance on the edge of her awareness. Sam was right. He was nothing like her father. Her father had been an angry, loveless man who vented his frustration and fury on a meek, unprotesting child. She had never defended herself against him; she'd merely retreated into a silent, miserable world.

Her encounters with Sam hadn't been like that.

She had given as good as she got, matched him word for word. She hadn't slunk meekly away. In these past nine years, she'd changed. She'd grown up and grown strong. Neither her father nor any other monster had power over her. An old ghost had been exorcised.

Her father hadn't loved her and that was sad. Sad for her, sad for him. But that was in the past. Sam did love her. Warts, witching stick, and all. So what if he did think she was a little flaky? After today, he'd have to rethink his skepticism. But since she'd repeatedly turned him away, would he give her another chance? She'd give almost anything if he would call or suddenly appear at her door, demanding to be let in.

She picked up her guitar and caressed the smooth wood. Strumming a few chords, she began to sing, thinking of Sam, willing him to come, drawing him to her with the power of her love.

Green, green, Guadalupe-green
Willow water wise.
Green, green, Guadalupe-green
It's the color of your eyes.

Max sat wishing with every fiber of her being that Sam would magically appear as the words became an emotional plea.

Now your arms enfold me
Come close to me and hold me . . .

She stopped, listening. The only sound she heard was the steady hum of the refrigerator and canned laughter from a television playing in the room next door. She sighed and laid the guitar aside. Such things only happened in romantic movies anyway.

Sam had pride as well, and she'd been so blinded by her own needs that she had trampled his once too often. He'd told her he'd be waiting. The next move was up to her.

A mischievous smile lifted her lips as a plan formed in her head. She jumped up and quickly dressed in dark slacks and a red sweater. After stepping into her loafers, she made up her face, pulled on her windbreaker, and stuck a flashlight into her pocket. Still chuckling, she dashed out the door and ran smack into a young woman who was about to knock.

"Sorry," Max said, stepping back into the room. "I was in a hurry."

"Are you Miss Strahan?"

"Yes."

"Oh, thank heavens I caught you. This is for you."

The young woman hoisted her delivery from where it was propped against the wall and brought it inside. Five feet tall and supported on a tripod, the thing was shaped like a giant wishbone and covered with white orchids and tiny green and blue glitter butterflies. Across its width was a white banner with CONGRATULATIONS in gold letters.

"I would have just died if I'd missed you," the harried woman said. "I hope you like it. Our shop has never made a witching stick before, but Mr. Garrett was very emphatic about what he wanted when he called this morning. I promised to have it at your door this afternoon, but we had to send to Austin and San Antonio to get enough orchids and the shipment was late. Then my assistant fell off a stool and hurt her arm and I had to take her to the hospital. I thought the doctor never would get there. Then wouldn't you know that my van wouldn't start, and I had to get somebody to come out and jump my battery." She took a deep breath. "It's been one of those days."

Max bit back laughter as she nodded sympathetically. "I've had those myself."

"I hope Mr. Garrett won't be angry that it was so late."

"It's fine," Max assured her. Then a comment the florist had made sank in. "Did you say that he called this morning?"

"Bright and early. The phone was ringing when I opened the shop."

After the woman had gone, Max unpinned the card from the ribbon and read it. "Congratulations, my lovely water witch," it said. "I'll be waiting."

He had placed the order before they'd hit water. She touched the velvety petals of the orchids and ran her finger over the sparkling wing of a green butterfly. "Sam Garrett, you dear, sweet man."

There was no moonlight to illuminate her way as Max parked beside the road and walked up the rise to Sam's. A steady chirr of crickets and frogs blended with the river's rush along its rocky path to muffle the sound of her footsteps. Keeping to the side of the drive so that her approach would be hidden by the trees and bushes, she stealthily picked her way toward the house.

Stumbling over a root, she fell to her knees and let out a soft curse. She got to her feet and pulled out the flashlight. She hadn't wanted to use it, but perhaps if she kept the beam pointed just a foot or two ahead of her, nobody would see it.

The porch light was on, but she didn't plan to use the front door. When she lost the cover of the trees, she turned off the flashlight and crammed it into the pocket of her windbreaker. Crouching low, she made a dash for the part of the house where Sam's bedroom was located. Once there, she plastered herself against the stone wall, concealing herself in the shadows and biting her lip to keep from giggling.

After a moment, she tiptoed toward the double windows of Sam's room and, moving very slowly, peeked around to look inside one. Except for a faint illumination from the hall, the room was dark. She eased over and tried the sash. It inched upward. Quietly, she raised it higher and threw one leg over the sill.

A hand clamped around her ankle. "I thought you'd never get here," a husky voice said from the darkness. Strong arms lifted her through the opening. "I've been waiting."

"Oh, Sam," Max said, disappointed that her ruse was foiled. "How did you know it was me?"

"For one thing," he said, gathering her in his arms and nuzzling the side of her neck as Dowser rubbed against her legs and licked her hand, "your friend here has been dancing around the house having a fit since you got out of the jeep. For another, you'd make a lousy commando, sweetheart. I saw your flashlight and you were about as quiet and unobtrusive as an elephant."

"An elephant!" She was indignant at the comparison.

"A very cute little elephant." He laughed and kissed her nose. "But noisy."

She joined in his laughter and snuggled close, relaxing against the solid warmth of him. It felt so good to have his arms around her. "How I've missed you." For a moment they simply held each other, eyes closed, pulses adjusting to a fast, synchronized beat. "Goose and I hit water. Seventy-eight-and-a-half feet."

"I know. Buck called me. I think that's wonderful, Angel. I'm so proud of you."

Smiling contentedly against his chest, she said, "And my agent sold some of my songs for an album."

"Fantastic." He gave her a little squeeze. "I never doubted that it would happen. You're very talented."

Dowser whined and tried to nudge his way between their legs. Sam switched on the table lamp and took the Doberman by the collar. "Come on, fellow. You've been romping with your girl all day. Now I want to do a little romping with mine."

Max knelt and hugged the dog, scratching his ears and saying a few words of greeting before Sam put him out and shut the door.

As he ambled back across the room, Sam's gaze devoured her. "Lord, woman, you look good. Come here to me." Grabbing her in his arms, he hugged her tight and rocked her back and forth. "I'm never going to let you out of my sight again."

"Oh, Sam, I have so much I want to say to you, so much I want to explain."

"Angel, there is only one thing I want to hear. No, make that two. I want to hear you say you love me. And I want you to promise that we'll get married as soon as possible."

Max looked up into river-green eyes shining with warm adoration, and her soul soared. "I love you, Sam Garrett. With all my heart. And I promise that we'll get married as soon as possible."

"That's my Angel."

His lips met hers and their spirits merged in a kiss that was sweeter, more potent than the rarest aphrodisiac of the gods. Old remnants of the past were swept away by wondrous new feelings as she clung to him, savoring the taste of his mouth, reveling in the feel of his hands on her body.

When he stopped to toss her jacket aside and lift her sweater over her head, she said, "Sam, I was so wrong about some things. We need to talk."

"Later, love, we'll talk later. I'm so hungry for you, I could die." He bent to run his tongue along the curve of her shoulder as his hands unhooked her bra, then slipped down to fumble with the button of her slacks.

"Sam," she said in a breathless sigh as her slacks slithered down her legs, "why did you order flowers sent before we finished the well?"

"Because, Angel, I believe in you." He scooped her up in his arms and walked toward the king-size bed. "And I went for broke."

THE EDITOR'S CORNER

We have some deliciously heartwarming and richly emotional LOVESWEPTs for you on our holiday menu next month.

Judy Gill plays Santa by giving us **HENNESSEY'S HEAVEN,** LOVESWEPT #294. Heroine Venny McClure and a tantalizing hunk named Hennessey have such a sizzling attraction for each other that mistletoe wouldn't be able to do its job around them . . . it would just shrivel under their combined heat. Venny has come to her family-owned island to retreat from the world, not to be captivated by the gloriously handsome and marvelously talented Hennessey. And he knows better than to rush this sweet-faced, sad-eyed woman, but her hungry looks make him too impetuous to hold back. When the world intrudes on their hideaway and the notoriety in her past causes grief, Venny determines to free Hennessey . . . only to discover she has wildly underestimated the power of the love this irresistible man has for her.

Two big presents of love are contained in one pretty package in **LATE NIGHT, RENDEZVOUS,** LOVESWEPT #295, by Margaret Malkind. You get not only the utterly delightful love story of Mia Taylor and Boyd Baxter but also that of their wonderfully liberated parents. When Boyd first confronts Mia at the library where she works, he almost forgets that his purpose is to enlist her help in getting her mother to cool his father's affections and late-blooming romanticism. She's scarcely able to believe his tales of her "wayward" mother . . . much less the effect he has on her. Soon, teaming up to restrain the older folks, they're taking lessons in love and laughter from them!

Michael Siran is the star twinkling on the top of the brilliantly spangled **CAPTAIN'S PARADISE,** LOVESWEPT #296, by Kay Hooper. Now that tough,

(continued)

fearless man of the sea gets his own true love to last a lifetime. When Robin Stuart is rescued by Michael from the ocean on a dark and dangerous night, she has no way of knowing that it isn't mere coincidence or great good luck that brought him to her aid. Indeed, they are both deeply and desperately involved with bringing the same ruthless man to justice. Before love can blossom for this winning couple, both must face their own demons and find the courage to love. Join Raven Long and friends for another spellbinding romantic adventure as "Hagan Strikes Again!"

You'll feel as though your stocking were stuffed with bonbons when you read **SWEET MISERY,** LOVESWEPT #297, by Charlotte Hughes. Roxie Norris was a minister's daughter—but certainly no saint!—and she was determined to win her independence from her family. Tyler Sheridan, a self-made man as successful as he was gorgeous, owed her father a big favor and promised to keep an eye on her all summer long. But Tyler hadn't counted on Roxie being a sexy, smart spitfire of a redhead who would turn him on his ear. She is forbidden fruit, yet Tyler yearns to teach her the pleasures of love. How can he fight his feelings for Roxie when she so obviously is recklessly, wildly attracted to him? The answer to that question is one sizzling love story!

You'll love to dig into **AT FIRST SIGHT,** LOVESWEPT #298, by Linda Cajio. Angelica Windsor was all fire and ice, a woman who had intrigued and annoyed Dan Roberts since the day they'd met. Conflict was their companion at every meeting, it seemed, especially during one tough business negotiation. When they take a break and find a baby abandoned in Dan's suite, these two sophisticates suddenly have to pull together to protect the helpless infant. Angelica finds that her inhibitions dissolve as her maternal qualities grow . . . and Dan is as enchanted with her as he is

(continued)

filled with anxious yearning to make the delightful new family arrangement last forever. A piece of holiday cake if there ever was one!

There's magic in this gift of love from Kathleen Creighton, **THE SORCERER'S KEEPER,** LOVESWEPT #299. Never has Kathleen written about two more winsome people than brilliant physicist Culley Ward and charming homemaker Elizabeth Resnick. When Culley finds Elizabeth and her angelic little daughter on his doorstep one moonlit night, he thinks he must be dreaming . . . but soon enough the delightful intruders have him wide awake! Elizabeth, hired by Culley's mother to look after him while she's on a cruise, turns out to be everything his heart desires; Culley soon is filling all the empty spaces in Elizabeth's heart. But healing the hurts in their pasts takes a bit of magic and a lot of passionate loving, as you'll discover in reading this wonderfully heartwarming and exciting romance.

It gives me a great deal of pleasure to wish you, for the sixth straight year, a holiday season filled with all the best things in life—peace, prosperity, and the love of family and friends.

Sincerely,

Carolyn Nichols

Carolyn Nichols
Editor
LOVESWEPT
Bantam Books
666 Fifth Avenue
New York, NY 10103